MW00827581

THE PRESIDENT'S GIRLFRIEND 2: HIS WOMEN AND HIS WIFE

MALLORY MONROE

ISBN:0615572839
ISBN-13:978-0615572833

COMING SOON
MORE INTERRACIAL ROMANCE
FROM
MALLORY MONROE:

DUTCH AND GINA

ALSO
ROMANTIC FICTION
FROM
AWARD-WINNING
AND
BESTSELLING AUTHOR

TERESA MCCLAIN-WATSON

AFTER WHAT YOU DID
DINO AND NIKKI: AFTER REDEMPTION
STAY IN MY CORNER

Visit
www.austinbrookpublishing.com
for information on all titles

ONE

They would not let up. Every question was an indictment. Every answer seemed wrong. And they kept on firing: How many students have been captured, sir? Why haven't they been released? Is Al-Qaeda involved? Why can't you give us more information, sir, after three long days? Why is your administration dragging its feet? What is your administration doing to bring our boys and girls safely home?

Walter "Dutch" Harber stood behind the podium in the East Room of the White House and answered every question with the coolness he was known for. The room was packed with wall to wall reporters, many drained and overworked, all roaring like lions of opposition, determined, it seemed to him, to treat this unfolding hostage crisis as if it could be that one big story that could bring his presidency down.

And here he stood, in that lion's den, equally determined to maintain his cool. He certainly looked the part, more than a few reporters had already commented to each other, as he stood there in his pristine tailored dark blue suit, his polished Italian dress shoes, his jet-black hair slicked back in a way that highlighted the smoothness of his forehead, his wide, sexy jawline, his eyes that were so green they looked like jade. And in that calm, confident look of his he managed, even in the mist of their swirling accusations, to exemplify a startling contrast to their loud, raucous scruffiness.

"I will say again," he said for what seemed to him to be the hundredth time. "The United States does not, and will not, negotiate with terrorists."

"But what if Al-Qaeda kills those students, sir?" the AP reporter asked in follow up. "According to our sources, they're demanding the release of Ben-al-Alawaiki or they will kill those students. Are you going to let those students die, Mr. President?"

"It has not been confirmed by my administration what organization is responsible for the abductions, so I don't know where you're getting this information about Al-Qaeda's demands. At this point we can't even confirm how many students have been abducted. And if, let me repeat *if*, Al-Qaeda is responsible, they would be well advised to understand what it would mean for them if they harm any of those American citizens. But again, we will not negotiate with terrorists."

When he refused to deviate from his theme, when he refused to slip up and say something unscripted about the hostage crisis that the cable news channels would have a field day criticizing, the press moved on. But their next target, as it had been ever since he started dating her and spiked to frenzied proportions after he married her, was Regina Lansing-Harber.

"Your wife, sir, gave an interview over the weekend where she said she'll continue to focus on social justice issues in her role as First Lady. She even questioned the laws of our land, saying that many of those mandatory minimum sentencing guidelines are the very reason why a disproportionate number of African-American males are incarcerated. She said those laws were unjust on their face. Why is your wife soft on crime, sir, and does that mean you're soft on crime also?"

The nerve of these people, Dutch thought with some degree of anger, although his face revealed nothing. "My wife is a trained criminal defense attorney," he calmly pointed out. "She's a professional who has been involved in social justice issues for well over a decade. She wasn't speaking randomly or off-the-cuff. She was speaking as a woman with considerable experience and expertise in the area in which you cite."

"But she blamed the laws on the books, sir, rather than the criminals themselves, for their incarceration. You didn't answer my question. Why is she soft on crime?"

"She's not soft on anything," Dutch said with a smile, although he was raging inside. He needed a release, and knew he would have to find that wife of his and get one as soon as this *inquisition-masquerading-as-a-press-conference* was over.

But it would be nearly fifteen more minutes of back and forth before Allison Shearer, his press secretary, could shout *Last question!*, he could answer it, and then he and his staff could leave that press room and that unrelenting press behind.

"That went well," Dutch said snidely to Max Brennan, his chief of staff, as Max scurried to keep pace with his taller, more athletic boss. A train of presidential aides followed closely behind the fast-moving men.

"We don't even know who the kidnappers are yet," Max said, virtually out of breath, "and they're already demanding answers. Geez. And now Congress wants to parade you up on Capitol Hill like some guinea hen so they can get in on the *Blame Dutch Harbor* bandwagon too. Which reminds me," Max said, stopping Dutch's progression by gently touching him on the arm. The aides, understanding, stayed back far enough to allow the two heavy hitters some degree of privacy. "The Congressional Hispanic Caucus wants to deal."

"Do they now?" Dutch asked. "That's some good news."

"Yes, sir, but they want a parade too. They're willing to offer public support for the Hearn Amendment only if you'll agree to a day-long summit here at the White House, cameras rolling, on immigration reform."

"An all day summit?"

"All day. I know it's crazy, sir, but that's their bottom line. And they don't mean a hello-goodbye by the president, either. They want you to chair the event so it'll get maximum coverage."

Dutch just stood there as he often did when his mind was deep in thought. He knew it would be virtually impossible to give any one event an entire day of his time. But he also knew that amendment would fail if he did not have CHC support. "If we can set it up, okay."

Max sighed relief. "Good. It won't be any time soon, I'll make that clear, but at least we can get that amendment out of committee."

"Set it up," Dutch said, about to continue moving. But Max stopped his progression again.

"Another thing, sir," he said, in a voice even lower. "Jennifer wants a meeting."

Dutch shook his head. "No."

"But, sir, she's the wife of a billionaire. She's one of the Democratic Party's staunchest supporters. You can't say no to one of our most generous donors."

"I thought I just did."

"What I mean is, sir, we have tough mid-terms coming up in a couple years, with some serious collective bargaining and other ballot initiatives we've got to fight tooth and nail. We'll need her money and the money of every donor we have on the books just for our ground game to be competitive, or we could lose those initiatives and the House could swing back into Republican hands."

"The answer is still no, Max."

"But why for crying out loud? Because you and her fooled around back in the day?"

"Yes," Dutch admitted. "But not just back then."

At first Max didn't get it. He frowned. "I knew you two had a thing going when you were in the Senate, but I don't see where. . ." And then he began to understand. He stared at the president. "Are you telling me," he started, and then forced his voice even lower. "Are you saying that you've been with her, *intimately*, since you've been president?"

Dutch hated to admit it. "Yes," he said.

Max could not believe it. He knew Jennifer Caswell was a great looker and there was a time when Dutch couldn't keep his hands off of her. But when in the world did Dutch hook back up with her? And why, Max wondered, was he always the last to know?

"When did all of this happen?" he asked the president, who also happened to be his best friend since childhood. "Was it since you've been with Regina?"

"No," Dutch said snappishly, finding the entire conversation disagreeable. "Of course not. Before Gina."

"But more than one time?"

Dutch nodded. "Yes."

"But," Max still wasn't quite understanding this. "She's married, sir. She was married during your first term."

Dutch looked at Max with great frustration, although his anger was more a reflection of his own disgust with the womanizing man he used to be, than any negative feelings he held toward his chief of staff. "I know she's married, Max, why are you telling me that?"

"I thought you didn't, even in your most active days, I didn't think you would fool around with a married lady."

"She married Ralph Caswell in some private, secret ceremony and forgot to mention it to me. Did we have sex while she was married? Yes, we did. Did I know she was married while we were having sex? No. Not initially, anyway. When I did find out I wish I would have immediately broke it off, but I didn't. Jen was a sexual habit for me by then and unfortunately, I wasn't able to break the habit that easily."

Max had heard about Jennifer's freakishness in bed, that was why, he believed, Dutch was interested in her to begin with. "So you guys continued to see each other after you discovered the truth?" he asked him.

"A few more times, yes," Dutch admitted, "until I became so disgusted with myself that I could hardly look at myself in the mirror. Then I broke it off. For good."

Max looked at his boss doubtfully. Jennifer Caswell was always one bad mood away from being certifiably nuts. For her to give up a man like Dutch Harber just because she got married to some rich old guy with plenty of dough didn't even sound like her. "And she just accepted that break?" he asked Dutch.

Dutch's eyes glazed over, remembering that crazy time. "Hardly," he said. "I had to literally threaten to tell her brand new husband just to get rid of her. And that's why I have no intentions of seeing her now." Then he frowned. "Anyway, I need to talk to my wife before we head over to Capitol Hill," he said, walking away, his aides now scurrying to follow behind him. "And get Ed Drake," he added without turning around. "I want a briefing on the ride over."

"Yes, sir," Max said as he watched him hurry to get to his wife. How a man like him could go from *Wham Bam Harber*, the love'em and leave'em specialist, to somebody completely devoted to that wife of his, was a mystery to Max. Especially considering that wife of his. Not that he had anything against black women, he didn't. He found them just as attractive as any other woman. But the one the president had decided to latch onto was just too black: dark skin, full lips, voluptuous body, hair either braided or in some other Afrocentric style that irked Max no end. And she was unapologetic about her style too, even when many national magazines, except maybe for *Jet* and *Essence*, constantly complained about her lack of taste. She just didn't seem to care.

And now Jennifer Caswell was back on the scene, a woman who once held Dutch's full attention. And held it, to Max's dismay, even after she married billionaire industrialist Ralph Caswell. That could be a problem. Not just for Dutch, not just for the Democratic Party. But for Max, who was secretly positioning himself to seek public office himself in a couple years. What if Jennifer was still in love with

Dutch, his ex's never seem able to completely let him go, and that was why she was insisting on this meeting? Dutch was no longer interested, and was making it clear, but what if she was still interested? That could be a nightmare, just like Kate Marris had been a nightmare. Jennifer had the kind of forceful personality that could create all kinds of havoc for the president.

Max began walking again, sighing as he walked. He knew he had to keep a lid on any more bimbo eruptions, not just for the president's sake, not just for the party's sake, but for his own as yet unspoken, but secretly very real political ambitions.

Max's assistant hurried up to his now-mobile boss. "You okay, sir?" he asked him.

Max frowned, looked at his subordinate with contempt. "Of course I'm okay! What are you asking me that for?" he asked him, his eyes unable to shield what he could just sense was a fast approaching storm.

Regina Lansing-Harber stood in the marbled shower stall inside the White House residence for far longer than it took to clean her already clean body. But she couldn't stop thinking about this new, in the fishbowl, under the microscope, in your face life of hers. Dutch had warned her repeatedly. He had told her not to expect any degree of reasonable treatment from a DC press corps that feeds on unreasonableness. And she had smiled; hit him playfully on the arm, as if he had told her some distasteful joke.

But she wasn't laughing now.

Dutch's inauguration for his second term as president was barely a month old and already they were on his case: blaming him for the weak U.S. economy. Blaming him for the stagnation in the European markets. Blaming him for the abduction of those silly-ass, risk-taking rich college students who chose to spend their winter vacation in a war zone of all places, a *war zone*! And now Dutch, who had too much on his plate already, was forced to clean up that mess too.

She leaned her head back and allowed the fierce stream of water to medicate her tense, black body, her hair freshly braided in small, neat rows dropped along her back. Although she loved Dutch dearly, she hated Washington and everything it stood for. They twisted and turned every statement, joked about every movement, loved to criticize her as if they were still sore that he didn't marry some beauty queen from Nantucket, but an African queen from Newark. And all of it, the gamesmanship, the got-cha questions, the ridiculousness, was beginning to rattle her.

She stepped out of the stall, not at all certain if she was ready to face another day in the hot seat, when she realized she wasn't alone. Her husband was standing there, his hands in his pockets, his tired, gorgeous body leaned against the doorjamb of the bathroom's wide entrance. She stared at him, and he stared at her, both worried sick about the other, about the stress the outside world constantly put on their brand new marriage, but both trying to get through it.

"I thought you were still at the press conference," she said as she watched his tired green eyes scan the length of her wet, naked body. He had worked so late into the night last night that he didn't even come to their bed, but opted, as he often did when he finished extremely late, to sleep in the connecting room. His running explanation, which infuriated her and she often told him so, was that he didn't want to wake her.

But she inwardly believed there was more to it than that. She believed that the demands of the job weighed so heavily on him that some nights he just couldn't face her. On those nights he didn't even sleep, but tossed and turned and worried himself sick until daybreak. And he didn't want her, or anybody else, to see him in such a debilitating state.

"It just wrapped up," he said.

"How did it go?"

He sighed, which she knew meant not good, pushed his muscular body off of the doorjamb as if he had to will himself to move, and walked toward the towel rack. She came toward him as he sat on the vanity chair. He wrapped her in the thick towel and began drying her off. "Almost every question was about the hostages and when will the mighty U.S. government, better known to the press as the inept Harber Administration, bring those wonderful kids safely home."

"Wonderful my ass," Gina said and Dutch laughed. "But for real, Dutch, who would go into a war zone, Afghanistan no less, when they know those people hate us and are trying to kill us? I mean, *who does that*? Rich idiots, that's who! And then their rich parents and the media want to blame you when you had nothing to do with it."

"I know, sweetheart," Dutch said, sitting her dried, naked rump on his lap as he began to wipe dry her inner thighs and womanhood. "But this is what I signed up for."

"That's true too," Gina had to admit, relaxing to the feel of his bare hand as it moved beneath the towel and began massaging her between her legs, flicking her clit. "But I still don't like it." Although she very much liked what he was doing to her. She leaned her face back, and he kissed her on the lips in a long, dragged-out, sensual assault that left her nearly breathless.

When she came back up for air, she asked the dreaded question: "What other topic came up during the press conference?"

Dutch was planting small kisses on her long, dark, sexy neck now. "One guess," he said as he kissed her.

"Ah, let me see," she said, enjoying his kisses. "Me?"

"Bingo," Dutch replied as he pressed her body even harder against his chest, his massaging fingers entering her now. He loved the way she was always so concerned about him, and hated that there was always so much to be concerned about. Sometimes, like now, as he removed the towel entirely and unzipped his pants, his massive rod already stiff and ready as it jutted out against her inner thigh, he wished he'd lost his reelection bid.

"I've got a meeting with the Republican caucus," he said, his voice becoming strained, "but I had to see you first."

"You had to *see* me first?" Gina asked with a grin. "Sure seeing me was all you had to do?"

Dutch smiled. "That too," he said as he lifted her bare feet onto his knees, his long rob now resting against her clit.

And then he opened her legs as wide as she could bear, and slowly slid in.

His breath caught the way it always did whenever he first penetrated her, as his penis made its way into a shaft so narrow, so tight, so wet and ready for his entrance that it took all he had not to ram it through.

He leaned back and closed his eyes, as he slid in and then out of her, as he gyrated in her, as his every movement reminded him of how much he loved this woman. For the longest time he slid in and out, forgetting that accusatory press corps and the rest of the world with it. And just enjoying Gina. Just enjoying his wife. He wrapped his arms around her naked body as he fucked her, as he refused to entertain anything else, except her.

Gina closed her eyes too as he gyrated her, as his thickness penetrated her womanhood and gave her that sweet, quivering feeling she always felt whenever he touched her that way. And as he slid so slowly, so expertly in and out of her, pleased that it won't be quick because they had never had quick sex in all of the times they'd been with each other, tears began to stain her lids. She loved him so much that it scared her sometimes. She'd never felt so strongly about another human being the way she felt about Dutch. He had supplanted all others in her life. He was now her father, her mother, her lover, her best friend. And a husband who couldn't be more attentive, even though the entire world demanded his attention too.

And she didn't know how to handle it. She tried to relax and just enjoy him, tried to divorce her mind from all of the craziness around them and let his penis do the thinking for her. But she couldn't entirely pull it off.

Even when he lifted her and carried her into their bedroom; even after he laid her on the bed, dropped his pants, and began fucking her as if he'd never had sex like this before, she kept thinking about the craziness of their life in a fishbowl.

And she kept thinking about shoes.

Her life had always been a rollercoaster ride. Whenever she was up, whenever she could kick her feet in the air and enjoy life in its fullest, something would happen to knock those feet back down. That awful hostage crisis after just a month into his second term had one shoe already knocked off, one foot already slammed down. And had her fighting with all she had to hold onto the other shoe.

She held onto her husband as he fucked her, as their sex-starved bodies turned a slow motion beat into highly-charged, high-arching thrusts. The thrusts seemed to heighten as he lay on top of her and wrapped her so tightly in his arms that there was no daylight between them. And he couldn't stop thrusting into her. It was more than a physical release for him. It was more than sex. It was a chance to leave it all inside of her, every bit of himself, as he grunted and thrust, thrust and grunted, until she understood that need.

And although she understood it more than he would ever realize, and was pleased once again by the perfect way Dutch knew how to do her, she couldn't stop thinking about those shoes. And about when, not if, but when the other one would decide to drop too.

But for now she did as Dutch had done and forgot all else, and just enjoyed the poking in and out, the thickness, the wetness, the hardness, the sheer magnificence of that rod.

TWO

Thirty miles off of the southern coast of Cape Cod, the helicopter circled and then landed along the outer edge of the Harber family compound on Nantucket Island. Jim Yerks, longtime family attorney, jumped from the craft and made the long trek across the lawn that led to the colonnade on the back side of the mansion.

Once inside the mansion, Nathan Riles, a sixty-seven year old black man who had been in the employ of the Harber family for nearly forty years, escorted him through the main hall, down a long, winding corridor, and then, after a cursory knock, into the morning room.

Standing at the lunette window was Victoria Harber, heiress to a tobacco fortune and the mother of the President of the United States. She was flustered, and anxious, and as soon as Nathan Riles deposited Jim Yerks and left, dying to hear the news.

"Was it her?" she asked with no pretense of disinterest.

Jim nodded. "It's her."

"But are you certain, Jim?"

"There is no question about it, Victoria. None. It's her."

Victoria put her hand to her chest, her hard blue eyes staring with a twisted hopefulness that turned

Jim's stomach. "What did she say? Did she agree to our terms?"

Jim walked over to her before he answered her questions. "She agreed to come forward, yes," he said, his long association with Victoria Harber more a reflection of his admiration of her deceased husband, than any affection he held for her. "But not for five-hundred thousand. As you rightly predicted, she wants more. She wants a million dollars."

Victoria snorted. "I knew that was all she was ever about. She never loved my son. Just wanted what he had. When I threatened to expose her, and showed her those sex tapes, she knew it was over. She knew he'd never want anything more to do with her once he viewed those tapes. But I still didn't expect her to agree this quickly."

"She's broke," Jim said. "She thought she was married to this wonderful, wealthy, French businessman when his so-called business wasn't worth the paper it was printed on."

"Oh, come now, Jimmy. You actually believe she loved that Frenchman?"

"I believe it, yes."

"Surely only because she thought he was rich."

"He *was* rich," Jim assured her. "Until the roof caved in. Until the authorities in Saint-Tropez caught up with his Ponzi scheme of a business. But by then she was deeply in love with the man."

"Now he's in prison and she's broke. Now she's ready to deal."

"She's ready," Jim said, "and you're ready. But is that son of yours ready?"

Victoria folded her arms, a gleam in her eyes. "If you only knew how much my son loved her, you'd understand my confidence. Yes, he'll be ready. He'll dump that black whore as quickly as it takes for him to fall into his real woman's arms. I assure you of that." She smiled. "He'll be ready. Don't you worry. He'll be ready most of all."

Jim, however, still couldn't wrap his brain around the motive. "But what I don't understand is why," he said.

"Why she accepted our terms?"

"Why you're offering them to begin with. Why you're willing to give a woman you obviously despise all of that money. We're talking a million dollars, Vicky. Even for you that's real money. Why would you be willing to give up that kind of cash?"

"I'll give up even more if I had to," Victoria stated with conviction.

"And what do you want from her in return?"

Jim immediately noticed that this question caused Victoria's hard blue eyes to sparkle. "Simply put," she said, "I want her to end my son's marriage. I want that farce of a marriage over before a child is produced. Because I'll accept a lot of things. I have accepted a lot from that son of mine. But I will not have *that* in my family. Not as an heir to my son's fortune. Not as any grandchild of mine. Do you understand me now? I'll not have that. I'll not have it!"

Jim stared at the mother of the President of the United States; stared at this liberal icon known the world over for all of her good work on behalf of the poor and disenfranchised. But if there was ever a more hateful woman, a more spiteful, dangerous woman, Jim Yerks had yet to meet her.

The limousine stopped in front of the DC Center for Social Justice in the heart of the hood and the press pool assigned to follow the First Lady were waiting in force when they drove up. Gina, dressed in an African-styled professional pantsuit, was seated in the backseat with Christian Bale, her husband's former personal aide. Christian had developed such a fond attachment to Gina that he had asked Dutch directly if he could become her personal aide. The president, who thought of the young, devoted, blue eyed, blond-haired Christian as a son, agreed. There was no-one else, he had said at the time, that he would trust more with his wife.

Also in the limo was Gina's assistant and best friend, Loretta "LaLa" King, a short, smart, outspoken woman on the verge of plumpness who used to be her business partner when they ran the Block by Block Raiders back in Newark. LaLa was Gina's girl, the one friend she knew she could always count on.

They all waited patiently for the secret service to give the all-clear so that they could step out.

"The vultures are circling," LaLa said as she glanced out of the dark tinted windows and saw the line of reporters waiting for them.

"I'm so over those reporters that it's not even funny," Gina replied, twirling around a bracelet. From her braids to her big earrings and beaded necklace, she was all Afrocentric today. A style LaLa loved. Her biggest fear, when Gina became First Lady, was that she would morph into some politically-correct, mainstream maven and would lose her own identity. A fear, LaLa was fast learning, that was completely unfounded. Gina was as much the same person today as she was when she said I Do.

"They can be appalling, can't they?" Christian said, his big smile lighting up his cherubim face. "I mean, they're doing their jobs and all, but good grief. They don't let up."

"I know," Gina admitted. "Now they're actually trying to blame Dutch for those students getting kidnapped."

"Ain't it crazy?" LaLa said, refusing to change an iota herself since becoming an assistant to the First Lady. "If those college students weren't rich and from Harvard, but was a bunch of Joe Blows from the hood, I'd bet they wouldn't be so obsessed with bringing them back home."

"I pray for their safe return, don't get me wrong," Gina pointed out, that sincere look her husband loved blanketing her face. "But to blame Dutch for those kids going over there in the first place? That's what I can't get over."

LaLa looked at her. "How is the President anyway?" she asked. "I saw him on TV this morning at that press conference, looking very gorgeous I might add. But they were brutal, girl."

"I figured as much. I don't even watch anymore. But he's doing okay." Then inwardly she smiled, remembering how Dutch took her to their bed after that press conference and made love to her so long and so hard that she still could feel the poke of that thick rod of his.

"How long have you known the president?" Christian asked her.

Gina smiled. "Why would you ask that, Chris?"

"Because y'all are so close. It seems like y'all had to have known each other longer than just last year."

"Oh. We met before then. Ten years before then."

"You knew each other for *that* long?"

"We had a one, we met briefly once, and then nothing for ten years, and then I was at the White House to get an award for Block by Block Raiders, and we hooked up again."

"Oh," Christian said. "And now you're in the fishbowl with him."

"More like a circus if you ask me," Gina said.

"The president has always been good with the press," Christian said. "He's used to the circus."

The door of the limo opened. "But I'm not," Gina said as she began to step out, "and I don't want to ever get used to anything this crazy."

As soon as her face was seen, photographers like paparazzi snapped their pictures and the press hurled their questions fast and furious. One reporter's voice, Nora Tatem from Slake magazine, was able to break through the chatter. "Mrs. Harber, why are you here?" she yelled.

Gina found her question so odd that she actually had to stop to answer. This, she viewed, was an opportunity to educate. She was wrong. "Why am I here at the Center for Social Justice?" Gina asked. "I'm here because this is a wonderful organization that helps the poor find competent legal representation."

"But is this an appropriate place for a First Lady to come?"

"Come on, G," LaLa whispered, gently taking her friend and boss by the arm.

"Why wouldn't it be appropriate?" Gina wanted to know, moving her arm from LaLa's grasp, her bright brown eyes riveted on the reporter.

"Isn't it obvious?" the reporter said.

"No, it's not obvious. Perhaps you can enlighten me."

"It's in the ghetto, ma'am," Nora Tatem pointed out and some of the reporters grinned.

"Yes, it is," Gina said, failing to see the humor. "But what's inappropriate about it? Because it isn't where the rich and well-connected are, I'm not supposed to come here?"

"Not unless you want to be referred to as the Ghetto First Lady."

Gina could hardly believe her ears. And this was Nora Tatem, a reputable reporter from a reputable magazine, not some tabloid yellow journalist.

"Because I'm visiting American citizens at an American Center in an American neighborhood that happens to be in a poverty-stricken area, I'm the *Ghetto* First Lady? Seriously?"

"Don't you think you're behaving low class ghetto right now, ma'am? For a First Lady, I mean?"

Gina's anger flared. "Oh, so because I called your ass out I'm behaving ghetto?"

"G," LaLa started.

But Gina would have none of it. "Because I didn't let you get away with your racist hogwash I'm low class?"

"Why are you dressed like that?" the same reporter asked.

Gina frowned, looked down at her professional pantsuit tailored with African Kitenge cloth. Then looked back up at the reporter. "Why am I dressed like what?"

"Like some African Jungle Lady." Again, laughter from some in the press pool. "Is that an appropriate way for an American First Lady to dress?" the reporter added.

"Come on, ma'am," Christian intervened, certain that this could quickly get out of hand. If it hadn't already.

But Gina was too amazed by the nonsensicalness of it. "So I can't wear an African outfit in America now?"

"Not unless you want to be the African First Lady."

Gina stared at the reporter who had a dead serious look on her face. "You sound like a fool, you know that?"

By now LaLa and Christian both had Gina well in hand, and was pushing, practically shoving her into the Center. A Center that erupted in applause as soon as the First Lady dawned its doors. But Gina, still reeling from her brief interplay with that reporter, once again couldn't stop thinking about shoes.

Dutch Harber entered the presidential limousine in a foul mood. Max, who got in behind him, and the president's National Security Advisor Ed Drake, who got in behind Max, could barely contain their anger too. It was noontime and they were still on Capitol Hill, preparing to head back to the White House, after a long and exhausting grilling from Congressional Republicans.

"Who do they think they are?" Max angrily wanted to know. "You're the president, gotdammit, not some two-bit Representative from some two-bit backwater town, and it's about time you let them know that, Dutch! I mean they wouldn't let up, demanding that you do this, that you do that. I couldn't believe it!"

"Even when I told them there's not enough credible evidence to officially link the abductions to Al-Qaeda," Ed Drake said, "they were still insisting that the president go before the American people and make it clear that we will not negotiate with Al-Qaeda."

Ed's cell phone began ringing.

"When he's already made clear that we won't negotiate with Al-Qaeda or any other terrorists," Max said as Ed answered his phone. "I tell you, Dutch, it took all I had not to slap the shit out of some of those Tea Party, tea-bagging conservative idiots!"

Dutch waved his hand. "Don't get your blood pressure up, Max, you know how the game is played. They're just trying to get some traction off of criticizing me. I can handle it."

"Well I can't," Max said, pulling out a bottle of pills and popping two. "I wanted to slap them, I declare I did!"

"Sir," Ed said, his cell phone against his chest.

"And if you would have slapped them, where would we be?" Dutch asked Max. Then he looked at Ed. "Yes, Eddie, what is it?"

"Turn on the television."

Max frowned. "What kind of thing is that to tell the president?"

"It's Allison Shearer, sir," Ed said. "She couldn't get through to your cell phone, Max. She says the president should turn on the news."

Max, knowing what a statement like that truly meant, quickly pressed the button that would turn on the limo's computerized television set, a set that allowed them to feed into cable channels as well. "Which channel?" he wanted to know.

"Which channel, Ally?" Ed asked into his phone. Then he placed it back on his chest. "She says all of them."

Max glanced nervously at Dutch as the television set came on.

And there was the First Lady of the United States, outside of some Center in what obviously was a rough part of DC, seeming to argue with well-known reporter Nora Tatem. Only it wasn't their full interchange, none of Nora's questions were shown, but only snippets of Gina's more aggressive responses:

"Oh, so because I called your ass out I'm behaving ghetto?" Gina was seen on television telling the reporter. And then another snippet:

"So I can't wear an African outfit in America now?"

And then finally:

"You sound like a fool."

And over and over those three snippets were being played.

"Please tell me it's not true," Max said, shaking his head in disbelief. "Please tell me not to believe my lying eyes. Please tell me I am not witnessing your wife, *our* First Lady, arguing with a reporter."

Max was staring at the television as he spoke. Dutch was staring too, but gave no comment. He, instead, changed the channel. From cable news outlet to cable news outlet, they were re-looping those same three snippets. Until he turned onto MSNBC, who played the entire interchange, including what Dutch could see were the reporters purposely inflammatory questions.

"That's what I thought," Dutch said.

"That's what you thought?" an increasingly perturbed Max Brennan said to his best friend. "What did you think?"

"I knew Gina wouldn't sprout out responses like that unless she was provoked."

"Who the hell cares about her provocation?" Max asked. "Look at her, Dutch! She's the First Lady of the United States! What First Lady in recent memory ever stood on national television and argued with a reporter? Name me one." He stared at his friend, his gray eyes troubled. "And she wonders why they treat her like some hood rat."

"Careful, Max," Dutch warned.

"But she acts like one, Dutch, I'm sorry but she does. Going to some rundown Center in the ghetto. What's she going there for anyway? What if there had been a drive-by shooting or something, and the First Lady gets caught in the crossfire?"

"Ronald Reagan wasn't in the hood when he was shot, so knock it off," Dutch said.

"And all of that African shit she's wearing--"

"Knock it off, Max," Dutch made clear, "or I'll knock the shit out of you!" He looked his old friend dead in the eye. "Understand me?"

Max glanced at Ed Drake, who was looking at him as if he could not believe he was talking to the president that way, best friend or no best friend. And then Max exhaled. "Yes, sir," he said. "I apologize, sir. But all I'm saying, sir, is that no matter how we try to spin this, no matter how we try to make that reporter the issue or that magazine she works for the issue or whatever: this looks bad."

Dutch didn't say a word. He didn't need Max or anybody else to tell him that. And then he turned the whole thing off.

Gina turned it on and watched reruns of those same three snippets over and over, until she could hardly bear it. She was back in the White House, in the East Sitting Hall of the residence, seated on the sofa with her feet tucked underneath her. With her were LaLa and LaLa's longtime boyfriend Dempsey Cooper, a tall, handsome, dark-skinned attorney who once was on the Block by Block Raiders board of directors. Gina had appointed him, as she had LaLa, to her White House staff. Demps, as they called him, was her deputy press secretary.

They all had drinks, with Gina nursing a Gin and bitters, as they watched the snippets over and over.

Finally LaLa had had enough. "Stop torturing yourself," she said as she grabbed the remote and turned the television off. "I was there. I know that's not how it went down."

"They make it seem like I was just snapping at that reporter for no reason," Gina said, her drink to her forehead as a low grain headache began to throb.

"The angry black woman," LaLa said. "Surprise, surprise."

"That's why you can't play into their hands," Dempsey said.

LaLa looked at him. "Play into their hands? Who's playing into their hands?"

"What I'm saying is--"

"No, I wanna know where you get off accusing G of playing into those assholes hands--"

"LaLa," Gina said, looking at her friend. "Just cool it, all right?"

"I'm sorry, G, but for him to say something like that. What's his problem?"

"What's your problem?" Dempsey wanted to know.

"I don't have a problem."

"And neither do I," Dempsey proclaimed.

"Stop it," Gina implored. "Please! I asked y'all to come to DC with me because you two are my closest friends and I knew y'all would have my back. But ever since we've been in this crazy town we've become stressed and tensed and I don't like what's happening to us. It's like we came here, determined to change this town, but this town is changing us."

Dempsey shook his head. "It's so much crap we have to take, G. You gave me the greatest job of my life, as your deputy press secretary, but the foolishness we have to respond to is unbelievable."

Gina agreed. "I know."

"We get Freedom of Information requests all the time about you, from all kinds of organizations, but you wouldn't believe the things they want. They want proof of your deceased parents' birth, as if they believe you never had any parents but was hatched from under some rock somewhere. One group wanted to see your high school transcripts, you, an accomplished attorney, as if you might not have graduated high school. It's ludicrous! And damned embarrassing too."

"You know what it's about," LaLa said. "Their great white father has married a black mother and some of them can't deal with that." Gina gave LaLa that look. Everything, in LaLa's world, seemed to trace back to race. Some of it did, Gina was no idiot, but *everything*? "I'm sorry, G," LaLa continued, "but even you know in this case it's true. So they bring on the dogs, sniffing for stuff. Like that reporter over at that Center. Now that's a problem."

'It wouldn't have been a problem if you would have done your job," Dempsey said.

LaLa looked at him. "What's that supposed to mean?"

"You should have gotten her away from that reporter, kicking and screaming if you had to, as soon as she made that first comment."

"How could you say something like that?" LaLa asked as she stared at her longtime boyfriend. She had always feared that DC would change Gina, but now she realized that her fear was misdirected. She and Dempsey, who could not have been more in love and closer before they came to DC to work for Gina, were now growing miles apart. "How could you fix your mouth to say something like that to me?"

"I'm just pointing out the obvious, La," Dempsey said. "It's your job to protect the First Lady from herself."

"Oh, I see. And how exactly was I supposed to do that? Drag her away from that reporter? Put her on my back and run down the road with her?"

"You dropped the ball, La," Dempsey made clear. "Don't try to act like you don't realize that."

"So it's my fault now? What that reporter did to G is on me?"

"That's enough," Gina said, too exhausted to even argue with them. "It's not on you or anybody else. I should have seen it coming. Now it's big news when Dutch has so much to deal with already. Now he has to deal with me and my blunders too. Everything I do he has to answer for, and I hate that."

The door to the sitting room opened and the topic of Gina's conversation walked in. Both LaLa and Dempsey stood to their feet as Dutch headed for the sofa.

"Good evening, Mr. President," Dempsey said.

"Hey, Demps, how you doing?"

"Great, sir."

"Mr. President," LaLa said.

"Hello, Loretta. You guys sit down, please."

"Thank-you, sir," Dempsey said just as LaLa was about to sit back down, "but we'd better run." Dempsey walked over to Gina, gave her a peck on the cheek. "Get you some rest, G," he urged.

"Thanks, Demps, you take care."

"You too."

Gina and LaLa hugged. "I'll call you later," she said, and then she and Dempsey, reigniting their argument, to Gina's dismay, were gone.

"Hey," Dutch said, staring down at his wife.

"Hey," Gina said, looking up at him. "I guess you saw the sound bites."

Dutch nodded. "I saw them."

"Max suggesting you divorce me?"

Dutch smiled weakly, unbuttoned his suit coat, and sat down beside her on the sofa. She immediately laid her head on his shoulder. He placed his arm around her waist.

"I felt so blindsided, Dutch. I thought she wanted to know about the Center. I mean, Nora Tatem doesn't have a reputation as an ambush reporter. But she sure ambushed me."

"You did nothing wrong, Regina."

Gina lifted her head and looked up at him. "What are you talking about? Every news outlet is criticizing me, saying I should have had more control of my emotions. Even the black press is upset with me. I just lived up to the angry black woman stereotype, they're saying. And you're saying I did nothing wrong? You don't think I behaved in a manner that wasn't befitting a First Lady, as CNN and FOX keep insisting?"

"I think you behaved fine under the circumstances. She provoked that altercation with her ridiculous questions. And the fact that you, as you put it, called her ass out, is what made it a story."

Gina stared at him. Could this man really be this good to her? "You mean you aren't upset?"

"With you? No. I'm glad you stood up for yourself, and I want you to continue to take a stand. Don't let this town ever take that away from you."

This town, Gina thought, and laid her head back on his shoulder. "Dutch, I was thinking," she started.

"Put it out of your mind, honey."

"Not what happened with that reporter. But about us."

Dutch's heart began to pound. "What about us?"

Gina hesitated, and then plunged on in. "I think it might be better if I was to leave Washington."

Dutch hesitated, fear gripping him. "Leave?" he said.

"Just until after your term in office is over. I was thinking about getting LaLa and Dempsey and going back to Newark, with the three of us running Block by Block Raiders again."

Dutch lifted her face up to his, his eyes staring into hers. "You want to leave me, is that what you're saying to me?"

"No, Dutch, not leave you. Just leave the situation for now. Just leave this town. I don't like it here. It's tearing my two best friends apart. It makes everything I do some kind of indictment of you. If I'm out of the fishbowl, at least the Washington version of it, maybe things will ease up for you. And then when your term is over we can try and live a normal life."

"But I just got sworn in for my second term a month ago, Gina. That's nearly four years you're talking about being separated from me."

"I can come and see you on the weekends, the way I used to do when we were dating."

"Are you out of your mind? I'm not seeing my wife only on the weekends!" Then he exhaled, to regain control, to ease the fear that continued to grip him. "It'll get better. I promise you it will. They'll move on to other things, they always do. Bashing my wife is just the flavor of the month for them right now. But please don't talk about leaving me."

There was such a plea in his voice that it startled Gina. She stared into his eyes. "Are you okay?"

Dutch tried to smile, but failed. "I'm okay. But please don't leave me, Gina."

Gina moved around and sat on his lap. Then she placed his gorgeous face between her hands. "I'll never leave you, Dutch. I promise you. I was just trying to make it easier for you."

Dutch pulled her into his arms, his eyes closing tightly. "Your being here, with me, has made it easier. You make it easier. Don't ever think that leaving me will make it easier for me, because it won't. Without you it would be unbearable, Gina."

Gina closed her eyes too. She hated politics, hated it with a passion, but would endure every political game they threw her way for Dutch's sake.

Then he stopped embracing her and looked at her, as if suddenly realizing something he must address. "I know they treat you horribly, honey," he said. "I read those press accounts. The racism in their coverage is so obvious that it sickens me. But if I didn't think you could handle it, I would send you back to Newark myself. But you're strong, Gina. You can handle this. I know you can."

Gina nodded. Her handling it was never the issue for her. "I know I can too," she assured him. "It's you I've been worried about."

"I'm okay," he said with a smile, revealing lines of age on the sides of his eyes. "There's just a lot of crap going on, that's all."

"And here I come with my nonsense."

"You didn't come with anything. That reporter took you there. That's why I ordered Max to have a conversation with her publisher."

Gina frowned. "But is that a good idea, Dutch? That publisher could claim we're trying to encroach on the freedom of the press or something."

Dutch smiled this time. "Don't worry, sweetie," he said, wrapping his arms around her again. "That's how the game is played around here. We complain, the publisher feels as if he's in the loop because he gets a phone call from the president's chief of staff, and he mentions it, off the record, to the reporter. Next time, the reporter, careful to keep her job, careful to please her publisher, is just a wee bit less aggressive. That's how it's done around here."

Gina shook her head. "Everything's a game. It's a wonder that anything gets done in this town."

Dutch stared deep into her eyes. "Promise me you'll never leave me, Regina."

Gina looked at him. She thought they had already established that. "I never said--"

"Promise me."

His seriousness concerned her. "I promise."

Dutch leaned her against him, as if a load had just been lifted. "Thank-you," he said.

Gina was distressed by his need for her reassurance that she didn't know what to say or what to do or how to make it clear to him that she was in this for the long haul. She decided to move on, to lighter matters. "Now that that's settled," she said, moving to rise from his lap, "I'd better get started."

"Get started?" Dutch asked, holding her back. "Get started doing what?"

"Cooking your dinner," she said, as she got off of his lap and headed for the kitchen.

Dutch, knowing how awful a cook his wife really was, panicked. "Gina, wait," he said, rising too. But Gina, knowing she wasn't about to cook anything, took off running, laughing as she went. Dutch, remembering the few meals she did try to cook for him and how dreadful each and every one of them were, took off running after her, terrified as he ran.

When he caught up to her, in the doorway of the kitchen, he grabbed her from behind. When he realized she was laughing so hard she was bent over, he smiled too. "You almost gave me a heart attack, child," he said.

Gina laughed even harder and turned around to face him. When she did, she could see that their nearness was beginning to affect his midsection. "Is my cooking really that bad?" she asked him, already knowing the answer.

"You were a good attorney when you worked as an attorney. You were an excellent businesswoman when you ran Block by Block Raiders. And now you're the perfect wife for me. But a good cook, darling, you *ain't*."

Gina smiled. "So it's like that, hun?"

"It's exactly like that," Dutch said, pulling her voluptuous body closer against his growing erection. "Although I failed to mention one other thing."

Gina stared into his eyes, moving even closer against his erection. She knew her husband well enough to know where he was going with this. "Oh, yeah? And what did you fail to mention?"

"That you're also very good, wonderful even, in bed."

Gina's heart started hammering. She placed both hands on the sides of his face, her big eyes narrowing as she gave him that earnest look of hers he loved so much. "I can't cook, but I can fuck, is that what you're trying to tell me?"

Dutch couldn't help but smile at the way Gina always managed to keep it real. "That's what I'm telling you. So," he said, his mouth moving slowly toward hers, "if you want to do something fantastic for this sex-starved husband of yours, why don't you do that which you're good at doing?"

43

His mouth pressed against Gina's and began kissing her in that slow, circular way she loved, with his tongue and her tongue soon adding to the circle.

And they kissed long and hard and repeatedly. They stood in the doorway of their private kitchen and kissed with a growing urgency that helped them to unload the stress and tension and craziness that swirled around them. To unload the remains of the day.

When he lifted her, and she straddled him, and he carried her into the bedroom, their kissing never for a second eased off. Because this was their moment, their chance to forget all else and concentrate on each other.

They continued kissing as he laid her on the bed and moved on top of her, wrapping her even tighter into his arms, still searing her with kisses he couldn't stop releasing. Until he had to release more.

He undressed her until she was completely naked, and he stared into those smoky brown eyes of hers until he had undressed himself and was naked too.

He knelt down at the bottom of the bed, opened her legs wide, and began to lick her between her thighs. It was gradual and tender, and Gina closed her eyes to experience nothing but the sensation of his touch. And as his tongue flicked and flicked her clit, the intensity caused her to release so much juice that he began to finger her, slipping into folds with one and then two fingers until she was so saturated that he knew he had to saturate her too.

He moved his chiseled body on top of her and entered her, gyrating inside of her in a perfect slow drag, making her feel heady every time his long, thick rod slid against her walls and then hit her spot. Over and over he did this, sliding deeper inside of her, and then hitting the bulls-eye with that preciseness that made her quiver. She moaned as he fucked her, as he kept sliding and hitting, sliding and hitting. Until he began to get thicker, and she took it all in.

Dutch laid his body down on hers as he began to expand to near explosion. And his once slow and steady gyrations became almost frenetic. This was more than just making love to his wife. This was more than just banging her, pounding her, fucking the shit out of her. Because he was doing all of that and more as he plunged into her, as he couldn't slow his pace again even if he willed it so. Because this wasn't about that.

This was about giving his all to her, to strengthen her against the madness she had to endure every day since becoming his wife. This was about reminding her that he would always be in her corner no matter what they threw her way. This was about *her*. That was why he kept staring at her closed eyes as he moved deeper inside of her. Staring at her exposed neck and radiant black skin and wondrously puckered African lips. That was why his face was beading with sweat as he fucked her; as he made it his mission to continually hit her where he knew she felt his sweetness the most. He wanted her to remember their togetherness in such fond sensuality that she would never again talk about separating herself from him, no matter what the reason. Because she just couldn't live without his sex. Because she just couldn't live without what she had to know was his total, complete, and undivided love.

Tears were in his eyes as he made love to his wife.

THREE

They all stood nervously when President Harber entered the Office of the Oval within the hectic West Wing of the White House. Present were what Max called the big three of the national security team: Secretary of State Gary Fecarra, Secretary of Defense Logan Winzieki, and General Matt Sullivan, Chairman of the Joint Chiefs of Staff. Max was also present, along with Allison Shearer, the president's press secretary. Dutch had called this meeting as part of his daily NIE, or National Intelligence Estimate briefing, and he wanted no more bull shit, Max had already warned them. He wanted answers.

Dutch sat behind his desk in the opulent Oval Office and immediately felt the weight of that office. He couldn't help but feel the weight as he sat behind what was historically known as the Resolute Desk, backed by a sweep of rich gold drapes, and fronted by an oval-shaped, presidential-sealed, pale gold rug of sunbeam design. Even above his head the ceiling bore a plastered replica of the magnificent presidential seal. It was the most impressive room in the White House, and Dutch kept it formal, as his team sat back down and provided answers.

Dutch sat back and listened carefully about possible threats around the country and the world, the terror alert warnings, and then the main issue: those hostages in Afghanistan.

His team spoke of every possibility, from military intervention, to an out-and-out covert operation, to sending in the SEALS in an effort to secure the release of those foolish college students.

The information they managed to piece together so far was so weak and contradictory that Dutch wouldn't even feel comfortable repeating it to the American people. The abductions occurred during an ambush of their convoy of cars that claimed many lives, according to his Defense Secretary, but the military couldn't even confirm how many students were already dead, how many were being held, or if they all were even adventure-seeking students, as the press seemed to believe. The working premise was that some Al-Qaeda operatives may be involved and that the hostages were possibly being held within some of the more populated, easier to hide-in-plain-sight regions of southern Afghanistan: Kandahar perhaps, Helmand Province more likely. But nothing was certain yet and there were no clear, easy answers.

Yet the press was demanding clearer, easier answers.

"When will we be able to at least confirm the number of students kidnapped?" Dutch asked Defense Secretary Winzieki.

"Soon, sir. We're reasonably certain it's seven, but we are not certain enough for you to go public with that number. However," he added, glancing at the Secretary of State which, Dutch knew, automatically meant that some new news had broke overnight, "we are now able to confirm that four businessmen were also abducted."

This astonished Dutch, not to mention his chief of staff. "Four businessmen?" Dutch asked. American?"

"Yes, sir."

Dutch's anger began to rise. "And when exactly were these businessmen taken and why were they in that war zone to begin with and why the hell wasn't I informed of this rather significant fact sooner?"

"They were on a fact-finding mission, sir," a now overtly nervous Defense Secretary said, "some kind of post-war business partnerships they were attempting to solidify, when their convoy came under attack and was ambushed yesterday."

"Yesterday?"

"Yes, sir, but we had nothing on it until early this morning, sir. Somehow their convoy had managed to get deep in the heart of Taliban territory so we couldn't even confirm that there was an ambush. And once we did confirm it, in the fog of war, we didn't realize that there were any survivals. It wasn't until very early this morning that we determined that four of the men survived and were captured. The Director of the CIA says our sources on the ground in Afghanistan do confirm that the four businessmen are being held along with the students."

"By Al-Qaeda?" Dutch asked.

Winzieki nodded. "We are not a hundred percent certain but yes, sir, we believe there's at least a loose affiliation to Al-Qaeda, yes, sir."

"Damn!" Max said.

"Which means, of course," Allison said, "that the press will insist that it's Al-Qaeda period. They will barely mention that *loose affiliation* fact."

"There's more?" Max asked, staring at the secretary of state.

Dutch looked from Max to the secretary. "What is it, Gary?" he asked him.

"One of the businessmen is Ralph Caswell, sir."

Dutch stared unblinkingly at his secretary of state. This couldn't be possible.

"Ralph Caswell?" Max asked. "As in the husband of Jennifer Caswell?"

The secretary of state nodded. "One in the same. When I heard it too, I was stumped. We can't possibly be this unlucky, I said. A billionaire? Are you kidding me? But we are just that unlucky this time. It's him. We were able to confirm it just this morning."

The secretary of state, and none of the national security team, knew of Dutch's prior relationship with the billionaire's wife. But even without that knowledge they knew having a billionaire as one of the hostages raised the stakes.

"Has she been notified?" Max asked. "His wife, I mean?"

"She believed it all along."

"She believed it?" Dutch asked. "Then why the hell wasn't I told anything about this *belief* of hers?"

The secretary of state looked at the secretary of defense, who, in turn, looked to General Sullivan, the Joint Chiefs chairman.

"We had absolutely no proof yet, sir," Sullivan said. "No proof-of-life video, nothing."

Dutch could barely take it all in. "Do we know where any of these people are being held?"

"We still believe it's around the Helmand Province, or possibly Kandahar, but these are only our educated guesses at this point. We haven't confirmed any of it. What we advise you to do is to keep making it clear that the United States will not negotiate with terrorists while we continue to get more consistent Intel."

Dutch, however, wasn't as firm about their advice as they were. "And what do you advise I do if these terrorists take to heart my repeated declaration that we will not negotiate with them? What if they determine they have nothing to lose and start dropping bodies on us, dead American citizens, since we're making it clear that we won't negotiate their release? What do you advise me to do then?"

All three men sat mute. "Yeah, that's what I thought," Dutch said, waving them away. "Okay, gentlemen, keep me in the loop, I don't care how trivial the Intel at this point. I don't want to be blindsided."

"Yes, sir," the men said, stood, and left.

Max and Allison stood around Dutch's desk, waiting for him to give instructions. Although they were not even cabinet level appointees, everybody knew that Max and Allison were the real power center of the White House.

"You will have to cancel your appearance at the G-8 summit in Brussels," Max said. "At least until this hostage crisis is over."

Allison agreed. "The nightly newscasts are beginning to count the days that the students, and now they will add the businessmen, including a billionaire, have been missing. *America Held Hostage: Day Four*, is the way they're playing it. The same way they played it when Jimmy Carter had that Iranian Hostage drama that was one of the issues that may have brought down his presidency. They're trying to compare you to Jimmy Carter."

"What else is new?" Max wanted to know. "Dutch won reelection and they still try to compare his administration to Carter's."

"Is that why she wanted to meet?" Dutch asked Max.

Max exhaled. "She wouldn't tell me at the time, but I've since confirmed, yes."

"Set up a meeting."

Max looked at Dutch. "Do you think that's wise at this point, sir?"

Dutch nodded. "Set it up."

"Here?"

"No. In the residence."

Max and Allison exchanged glances. "Yes, sir," was all Max could say to that.

Allison looked at Dutch. "Is she going to be a problem, sir?"

Dutch just sat there. Jennifer was so beautiful that she was one of those women most men automatically considered *got to fuck* material. But she always thought of herself as so much more. She married Ralph Caswell, a man in his sixties, because she was ambitious and wanted to be a billionaire's wife, but also because Dutch, the man she claimed she really wanted, wasn't making any moves in that direction. But her heart, from what he'd since been told, was always with him. Now, if he didn't play to her tune, he knew she could cause major difficulties for his administration.

Not to mention for his new, fragile marriage.

That night, after dinner, Dutch and Gina were playing a game of Chess in the White House billiards room. He watched her as she stared at the board, as her intelligent eyes seemed unable to quite know what move to make. Max had advised him to keep her out of it, to meet privately with Jennifer and see what she has to say before he even mentioned it to Gina. Jennifer, as Max well knew, was a selfish bitch who was never above making trouble for anyone, including the President of the United States. This could get messy, Max had warned, and if Dutch didn't want to add to Gina's reticence about being in DC in the first place, he'd be wise to keep her out of it.

"Perhaps you'll make your move before the end of the year," Dutch said mockingly to her.

Gina smiled. "Don't rush the master," she said as she continued to survey the board. Then she glanced up at him, saw that look on his face she was beginning to know so well, and looked back down at the board. "How did it go?" she asked him.

"How did what go?"

"Word around the House," she said, to Dutch's smile, "is that you had a meeting with the Big Three today, and that they had more bad news." She glanced at him again when she said this. By his hesitancy, she knew it was true. She stared at him. "What is it, Dutch?"

"They still don't know where the hostages are."

"Yeah, I already worked that one out. But what else?"

Dutch exhaled. "In addition to the seven students, there are apparently four businessmen being held."

Gina stared at him. "Confirmed?"

Now Dutch was staring at the board. He nodded.

"But--"

"And one of those businessmen is Jennifer Caswell's husband."

"Are you serious? The billionaire?"

Again Dutch nodded. "Yes."

"Dang, Dutch. This is getting out of hand. Are your people up to the job? What's the Defense Secretary telling you?"

"They're up to the job. It's a tough situation."

"And everybody's blaming you, but nobody's blaming those silly rich students."

"And now four not-so-silly businessmen."

"Why would they even be over there?"

"A fact-finding mission, according to Gary."

"In a war zone?"

"I know," Dutch said. "But there you have it." He stared at Gina. And he knew he couldn't take Max's advice.

Gina quickly picked up on his concern. "What is it?" she asked him.

"Are you busy tomorrow night?"

"No. Why?"

"I have a meeting with Jennifer Caswell tomorrow night. I want you to attend."

Gina didn't understand why, but she nodded. "Okay." She expected Dutch to explain. When he didn't, she asked.

Dutch leaned forward over the board, his elbows on his knees, the V-neck sweatshirt he wore tight across his muscular chest. "She and I used to be an item, Regina."

Gina stared at him. "An item?"

"Yes," he said.

Gina's heart began to race. "When?"

"We first got together when I was a senator. It continued during my first term as president."

"What do you mean got together? You and she were lovers?"

Dutch nodded. "Yes. But I broke it off after you and I became serious."

"But I thought you were seeing Kate Marris at that time."

Dutch placed both hands under his chin and began to rock unsteadily in his chair. "I was," he said, studying her reaction.

It didn't take anything more than that for Gina to understand exactly what he was saying. This man she now found so virtuous seemed to have been even more of a cad than she had assumed. "Why did you feel the need to see two women at once?" she wanted to know.

"They weren't . . . They were sex partners, Gina. Nothing more than that."

They stared deep into each other's eyes, until Gina looked away. Dutch's heart broke when Gina looked away. He hated that she had to know that side of him.

Gina looked at him again. "Why are you telling me this?" she asked. She was nobody's fool. Something more was at work here.

"Because I was seeing her just before you and I became an item--"

"Don't say it like that!" Gina said snappishly, the stress of her new life beginning to show.

Dutch's heart plunged. "I didn't mean it like that, Regina, you know I didn't. I never thought of you that way."

"Just," she said, not interested right now in his *but you were different* speech because she wouldn't be at all sure if he hadn't laid that same line on his other females. She frowned. "What were you about to say?"

"I was seeing Jennifer before you and I became serious, but the press may not see the difference. They may assume I was cheating on you, which isn't true. But I want you prepared should those kinds of questions come your way."

Shoes, Gina thought. *Shoes!* "Was she in love with you?" she asked, her eyes narrowing as she studied her husband.

Dutch hesitated on this question, which disturbed Gina even more. "It's my understanding that she was, yes."

"Were you in love with her?"

Dutch shook his head. "No."

Gina frowned. "I still don't understand. Why are you so concerned if it was nothing to you?"

"It was something to me; I'm not saying it wasn't. It was mainly a sex thing, but I also cared for her."

"But I still don't see why this old news is bothering you. What are you not telling me?"

Dutch exhaled. "She could pose some difficulty for me."

"But how? Because you used to bang her?"

"Because I used to bang her even after she was married."

This stopped Gina cold. She stared at Dutch. Dutch knew there was nothing he could say to sugarcoat a truth like that, so he remained silent.

Gina looked back down at the board, remaining silent too. What in the world, she sometimes wondered since marrying Dutch, had she gotten herself into? She knew Dutch used to have that playboy thing going. Wham Bam Harber, after all, used to be his nickname. But somehow she thought he would have been more honorable than that. Sleep around, yes, she knew he did that, but why a man with his obvious gifts in the bedroom would need to sleep with a married woman? The only answer, that he couldn't get enough of that particular woman, troubled her. And now he wanted her to meet this woman? What kind of town was this, she wondered.

"Regina," Dutch started but Gina immediately moved her Rook on the chess board. It was the wrong move, even she knew that, but at least, she thought with a kind of nervous sadness, she made a move.

"Honey, listen to me. Please."

Gina reluctantly looked at him.

"It was a terrible mistake," he said, "and we both knew it was."

"A mistake?"

"Yes," Dutch said.

"No," Gina insisted. "Spilling a drink on the carpet is a mistake. Forgetting to say I'm sorry when you bump into somebody is a mistake. Sleeping with another man's wife is no mistake, Dutch. You knew what you were doing."

"I didn't know she had gotten married initially."

"So when you found out," Gina asked pointblank, "did you then call it off?"

"No," Dutch had to admit. "Not right away."

"Why, Dutch?"

"Because we were already involved."

"Then why did she marry somebody else if y'all were so tight?"

"Because she's a shameless gold-digger and she knew I wasn't going to let her dig into any of my gold. All right?"

Gina looked so flustered that Dutch wanted to pull her into his arms. But she stood up before he got the chance.

"Gina," he said as he reached for her arm. But she pulled away from him.

"Gina," he called again.

"I'm all right, Dutch. I just need, I'm just going to go to bed," she said, leaving as she said it.

And Dutch watched her as she sashayed out of the billiards room, her entire body seeming to sag before his very eyes; sag with the weight of being his wife.

And because of it, because of his part in her pain, he didn't try to stop her. He let her go.

FOUR

It was a tough night all around. Dutch had to spend most of it in the Situation Room with his national security team, while Gina retired to the bedroom and stayed there. She was so emotionally drained, so unsure what to make of Dutch's "confession" that she just wanted to sleep it off. It was one thing when the press accused her husband of being a womanizer, but it was something entirely different when he confessed that he was.

It happened before she became his woman, and she understood that. It wasn't about that for her. What concerned her was the fact that he would continue to fool around with a woman after she had married somebody else, and this woman would let him continue to bang her, was what Gina couldn't get over. For this woman to continue their illicit affair after she was newly married, meant that she either didn't give a damn about her new billionaire husband, or that she had some mighty strong feelings for Dutch.

And although Dutch insisted it was just a sex thing for him, he also admitted that he cared for the woman. And now he wanted her to meet this woman? She fell asleep thinking about that, and wondering if there was more to this story than Dutch was letting on.

She, in fact, wouldn't see her husband again until that following night, just before the meeting was to take place. He slept in the guest room because he had stayed so late in the Situation Room, and by morning, when she did wake up, he had already gone to the Oval Office to begin his jam-packed day. Now it was evening again and she was relaxing with LaLa and Demps in the East Sitting Hall of the second floor residence. Christian was there too, but he was mostly on his Blackberry. Although she didn't share with them what Dutch had shared with her, they could tell that something mighty was bothering her.

"I'm okay," she insisted. "Just a little tired I think."

LaLa looked at her friend. She'd known Gina too long to believe that. "Yeah, and I'm Beyonce. What's going on, kid?"

"She said she was just tired, LaLa," Demps said. "I don't know why you're trying to make a federal case out of it."

"I know G, that's why. And I know something's bothering her. She may not want to share it with us, but it's there. It's sho' nuff there."

Dempsey rolled his eyes. Christian grinned. "Mrs. Harber told me about your psychic powers, LaLa," he said. Demps laughed.

"Very funny," LaLa said with a smile. But she continued staring at Gina. Christian, understanding, stood to his feet.

"I'd better call it a day, ma'am," he said to Gina. "Unless you still need me for anything?"

"Chris has a hot date tonight," Demps said, standing too.

LaLa looked at Christian. "Really, Christian? Who?"

Christian was suddenly shy. "Just a girl," he said.

Gina smiled. "Renita?"

Christian blushed, and then nodded his head.

"Good for you," she said. "And you are free to go and enjoy your evening."

"Thank-you, ma'am," he said, and hurried out.

"Hold up, man," Demps said, following behind him, "I want details."

When they were gone, LaLa looked at Gina. "Who's Renita?"

"She's one of the president's assistants. Really nice, attractive girl."

"Now back to you. What's brewing kido? And don't tell me nothing's brewing because I know it is."

Gina stood up and walked over to the fanlight window and looked out at the US Treasury building, the Jacqueline Kennedy Gardens, the East Colonnade. She folded her arms. "We have a meeting tonight."

"You and the president?"

Gina nodded.

"Who with?"

"Jennifer Caswell."

"The billionaire's wife?"

"Yes ma'am."

"Why would you need to be in that meeting? It's going to be about securing her husband's release, right?"

"That's my assumption."

"Then why you've got to be there?"

Gina exhaled. "Dutch wants me there."

"But why, Gina? Work with me, sister."

"Because," Gina said, turning her back to the window and facing LaLa, "she and he used to be an item."

"Oh," LaLa said, understanding immediately. Then she frowned. "But I still don't see why you would need to be in a meeting with her just because of that. I'm sure it was before he hooked up with you."

"It was. But . . . there's a little more to the story."

"Like what?"

Gina didn't normally tell her business like this, but living in DC and dealing with so much, she felt she had to tell somebody. And besides Dutch, LaLa was really the only person on earth she could talk to about something like this. "She may have been married at the time," she said.

"Married at the time of what?" LaLa asked, still confused. Then she understood. "Oh. The president and a married woman? Really? That's actually surprising."

"I know. I guess that's why it's so disturbing to me. I would have never believed it if he hadn't admitted it to me himself. So now I'm wondering what else don't I know about him?"

Knocks were heard on the door of the room. "Yes?" Gina called out.

The door opened and one of the household staff stepped in. "Mrs. Caswell has arrived ma'am," she said.

Gina looked at LaLa, this was unexpected, and then she looked back at the aide. "Please notify the president of her arrival," Gina said.

"Yes, ma'am," the aide said and stepped back out of the room, closing the door.

Gina walked over to the sofa. "Didn't expect her to come before Dutch arrived," she said as she sat down.

"I'm saying," LaLa said, and then stood to leave. "I'd better get away while I can. Go find out what Demps is up to. It could get ugly in here tonight," she added with a smile as she left.

Dutch arrived shortly after LaLa's departure, and as soon as he had come out of the bathroom after freshening up, Jennifer Caswell, escorted by Max Brennan, walked in. Only Jennifer didn't just walk in, she swept in. Her, the billionaire's wife, in her mink coat, mink hat, and mink-laced gloves. You'd think she just stepped off of a plane from Siberia the way she was dolled up, Gina thought. And that grand entrance surprised her too. She expected a worried, terrified wife, but instead this woman came across as rather fearless. Beautiful and fearless. Formidable even.

She walked up to Gina and Dutch, removing her gloves as she came. Her assistant, a tall, thin, nervous-looking young man, close behind her.

"Hello, Dutch," she said, handing her gloves to her aide, her narrow blue eyes seemingly fixated on Gina.

Dutch exhaled. He hated that she was somebody he'd been intimate with, hated that she had to be exposed to his wife. "Hello, Jennifer," he said. "Say hello to the First Lady."

Although Jennifer maintained her fierce look, Gina caught a quick glimpse of storminess within those eyes.

"Yes, of course," Jennifer said, extending her hand. "How are you?"

"I'm very well, thank-you," Gina replied, shaking her hand. "I'm sorry to hear about your husband."

"Oh?" she asked. "And what have you heard?"

"I mean about the kidnapping."

"I know what you meant," Jennifer said in an almost accusatory tone.

"Why don't we all just sit down," Max suggested.

Jennifer didn't bulge. "Thank-you, but no," she said, now turning her full attention to Dutch. "I'm here for answers."

"We're doing everything in our power," Max assured her, "to secure your husband's release."

"What specifically are you doing, Dutch?" Jennifer asked the president, her blue eyes blazing as she looked into his green ones. And Gina could just feel what she was thinking. Any woman who'd spent time in bed with Dutch and was no longer his woman, had to have regrets.

"The Defense Secretary," Max started, "has made it clear---"

"I'm speaking to the president," Jennifer made herself clearer. "What are *you*, Dutch Harber, leader of the free world, doing to secure my husband's safe return?"

That was one tough cookie, Gina thought. She was a woman to be reckoned with. And beautiful to boot, with that yesteryear, kickass, Farrah Fawcett vibe going for her. Gina understood Dutch's attraction to her, and she also understood why he wanted her to be here when they met again. Jennifer Caswell was a force of nature, something to be witnessed to be believed.

"I'm doing everything that can be done at this point to get all of the hostages released," Dutch told her.

"I offered them ten million dollars," Jennifer said without blinking an eye, "and they said no. They don't want my husband's money. They want the release of that prisoner at Guantanamo Bay, that terrorist, and they want him released now, or they will start killing hostages."

"We know what their demands are, Jen," Dutch said. "But what I want to know is why are you negotiating with them outside of the parameters that we've set up for all of the hostages? When my administration met with the families, my people made clear that there was to be no outside interference."

"Interference, hell, Dutch! They've had my husband for six days---"

What in the world was she talking about, Dutch thought? "What six days?" he asked. "He was captured yesterday---"

"No, he was not," Jennifer said. "But see? This is exactly the problem. You, the President of the United States, don't even know what your own administration is up to. And you can't say they didn't know about it because I notified the State Department myself as soon as I got that ransom note. The State Department told me to tell no-one, to sit tight, that they were already working on it."

Dutch looked at Max, which caused Gina to look at him too.

"It's true," Max admitted. "I just found out today myself."

Dutch frowned. "They why the hell did Gary tell me that cockinbull story about just getting the facts yesterday morning?"

"Apparently there was a communications glitch from the time Jennifer called, that's what the secretary told me. He said after Mrs. Caswell phoned, his chief of staff decided to keep it at the aide level until more Intel could be obtained."

"So it's the fault of his chief of staff?"

"I know," Max said, agreeing with Dutch. "That's the secretary trying to save his hide."

"I want him in my office as soon as this meeting is over."

"Yes, sir."

"What did the ransom note say?" Gina asked Jennifer.

Jennifer looked at her, looked her up and down, in fact, and then looked back at Dutch. "Again," she said, "what are you going to do to secure my husband's release?"

"What did the ransom note say?" Dutch asked her.

Jennifer almost glanced at Gina to see if she was gloating, but proved too much of a pro to show her hand that easily. "It said that my husband has been captured, and that I was to notify the State Department. If I was to notify any entity other than the State Department, he would be killed. That was six days ago. I requested a meeting with you only after the State Department kept dragging its feet, and then after those students were abducted I began to get seriously concerned. I called Gary; I called the secretary of state, that's how concerned I was. But when he wouldn't even return my phone calls, I asked for this meeting with you. Now, again, what are you going to do?"

"We are not going to release any terrorist," Dutch said point blank. "I can tell you that right now."

"Then here's what I'm going to do," Jennifer said. "I am going to hire a group of mercenaries. Your government will allow these men access to Gitmo, where they will take that terrorist my husband's captors are demanding, and give him to them in exchange for my husband and the other hostages, if they care to release the others."

This woman was nuts, Gina thought. She looked at Dutch.

"You know that's out of the question, Jennifer," Dutch said to her.

"Oh, I wouldn't speak so fast, Dutch."

Dutch stared at her. He once couldn't get enough of her. Now he couldn't stand the sight of her. "Are you threatening me?"

"Yes," she said. "And here's the threat: If your administration doesn't secure my husband's release, or at least allow me to secure it, I will expose you. And you know what I'm talking about."

There was a long hesitation in Dutch, which concerned Gina. Then he spoke. "Do what you have to do," he told Jennifer.

"A Family Values president who sleeps with married women could lose his moral authority, especially when I get through with him. And all of those millions of dollars Caswell Industries had planned to give to further all of those Democratic candidates and Democratic causes will go straight to Republican candidates and Republican causes if you drop the ball on this one, Dutch. There may even be cries for your impeachment when all is said and done, if you blow this one."

Dutch continued to give her his assessing eye. "Do what you have to do," he said again.

"Okay," she said, retrieving her gloves from her aide. "Don't take me seriously. But if anything happens to my husband," she said, putting on her gloves, "your time in office, if you even remain in office, will give new meaning to the term 'lame duck presidency.'"

And she and her aide were gone.

"She's broke you know," Max said and Dutch looked at him.

"She signed a prenuptial agreement. Ralph Caswell dies and she'll have nothing, or at least next to nothing. His grown children, who can't stand her, saw to that. That's why she's fighting so hard. It's richer for her to keep him."

"Well," Dutch said, still staring at the door Jennifer had just vacated, as if fearing that she would unceremoniously reappear, "at least I know where I stand."

Max agreed, although Gina wasn't at all sure. Because that woman, as they often said in her neighborhood, had trouble written all over her. Force of nature was right, because that was truly her. She came like the wind, but Gina felt as if it would be her husband, if he wasn't careful, who would get caught up in her whirlwind.

It wasn't until nearly midnight before Dutch could finish his meetings with his various administration officials and make it to bed. By then Gina was fast asleep. She had tried to remain awake and wait for him, but her body wouldn't cooperate. Besides, she assumed he wouldn't come to their bed at all, given the late hour, but would sleep in the adjacent room.

Dutch, however, needed Gina. He needed to hold her, to feel her, to lie next to her. So he did. He knew it was selfish on his part, he hated bringing his job to their bed, but he needed her too badly. And she did indeed wake up as soon as his weight bore down on the bed, as she always did, and he gathered her naked body into his arms.

"I'm sorry, sweetheart," he said to her, rubbing his lips across her forehead, his penis jutting limply against her vagina, "but I couldn't be without you tonight."

Gina snuggled closer to his naked body, rubbing her mound against his manhood. "I'm glad you couldn't," she said, kissing him back, thrilled to be in his arms.

They continued kissing for a good long time, but more in a series of pecks rather than one long, fluid passionate kiss. The elephant in the room was Jennifer Caswell and her threat to "ruin" him, as if there was more that she had in her bag of tricks than she was letting on, but neither broached the subject. They just kissed.

When Gina took Dutch's silky black hair that had fallen over his forehead and smoothed every strand out of his gorgeous face, she saw an understated but burning need deep within his big, green eyes that made her know instinctively what would cure that need. She turned her curvaceous body opposite his, her butt now pressed against his stomach. And he reacted immediately, sliding first his fingers into her folds, lubricating her, and then sliding his rod into her with a sureness that made her sigh in a loving relief, as she felt the touch of his head penetrate her folds.

He pushed into her with slow, prodding motions, his penis not in its usual instantaneous readiness, but requiring a longer, focused nurturing. But they both knew that his erection wasn't the issue this time. Their love was. The fact that they often felt as if it was the two of them against the world was what was driving their passion this time. And that was why they kept it slow, as Gina continued to lubricate them both. For the longest time they just lay there, as his penis slid gently into her wetness and then slid back toward her entrance tip, over and over again; as the lustful sound of their mating echoed with sloshing sensuality throughout the massive bedroom.

Gina closed her eyes as he made love to her. And Dutch closed his eyes too, that feeling of safety, of being with who he was supposed to be with, of knowing that the entire world may consider him and his administration a failure, but Gina would have his back. And just the thought of her, of her love and his love for her, lulled him into a peaceful, restful, unbelievably lustful fuck. They rarely did it this way, but it was needful tonight.

And even when they both eventually came to orgasm, it wasn't their usual mountain summit moment, but was more of a quiet, wonderful quaintness; the kind of release that spilled out in a drip rather than a splash, her folds tightening around his penis as he engorged, and she filled up, and both stretched out in a wonderful sweetness. A sweetness that bespoke of togetherness, of an unshakeable union, of a kind of quiet knowing that, despite the odds, they were both in this for the long haul.

Within minutes after their climax, they were both fast asleep.

But their peaceful sleep was barely an hour old when the president's secure telephone began to ring. Although it used to be known as the Washington-Moscow red phone during the dark days of the cold war, it was now known in the Harber Administration as the Hotline. And whenever it rang it was certain to be a call serious enough that the national security team deemed it worth waking the president over, even as late as three a.m.

Dutch, upon awakening, answered the call.

Gina woke up too, surprised to find that she was lying on top of Dutch. Sometime after she had fallen asleep, Dutch had apparently pulled her on top of him and rested her head against his bare chest. She looked up from that chest as he answered the call.

"This is the president," he said into the phone.

"It's Ed Drake, Mr. President."

Ed, the president's national security advisor, sounded almost solemn. "What is it, Ed?" Dutch asked him.

"The captors, sir, whom we are now certain is an Al-Qaeda affiliate, has killed a hostage."

The anguish swept through Dutch like a raging sea. He removed the phone from his ear, to steady himself, and then replaced it. "Who did they get?"

"Mary Beth Kappers, sir, a nineteen year old student."

Dutch closed his eyes, pinched his temple, and then reopened them. "Have they provided a message?"

"Yes, sir. They want us to know that they will continue to kill hostages if Ben-al-Alawaiki isn't released from Gitmo and placed into their hands immediately. That is their only demand and they're sticking to it."

"Can we get this Al-Alawaiki character to record a counter message condemning their tactics and making clear he'll refuse to go even if they win his freedom?"

"We have tried everything, and I mean everything, sir, to get him to do just that. But he will not. We could do a whole lot more, of course, if Congress hadn't tied our hands---"

"That's a fight for another day, Eddie. But do what you have to do. These are kids we're talking about. And keep me posted," Dutch ordered and hung up the phone. He wrapped his arms around Gina, who was still staring at him.

"What's happened?" she asked.

Dutch was so disgusted by the news that he first needed to compose himself. "They've killed a hostage," he finally said.

Gina deflated. "Oh, no, Dutch. One of the students?"

"Of course a student. They're terrorists; it's their job to terrorize. And they can expect far more outrage from the American public if they kill a bright eyed nineteen year old rather than some rich, middle-aged businessman. So they go for the shock value."

Gina's eyes studied his. "Are you all right?"

Dutch thought about this. "When this job is over, and I can take my wife as far away from this environment as I can possibly get her, yes, I will be," he said, and laid her head back down on his chest.

FIVE

The president stood behind a makeshift podium in the White House Rose Garden with the Prime Minister of Israel, Benjamin Shamir, flanking him. Given that it was the morning after the murder of a hostage, it was to be a simple photo-op, with the president thanking Mr. Shamir for his visit to the United States and the prime minister thanking the president for his friendship with Israel and his undying commitment to the Israeli-Palestinian peace process. No questions, they decided and had already alerted the press, would be taken. The assembled press, however, had other ideas.

Their questions came before the men could even finish their greetings. And not one of those questions concerned the peace process or how the prime minister was enjoying his stay in the United States. But every one of their questions concerned the hostage crisis and what they viewed as the president's lackadaisical response. It became so contentious that the leaders had to end their prepared remarks early, shake hands and give the obligatory camera wave, and then get ushered back into the White House as if they were being forced along.

One reporter, however, still was able to get in what would become the sound bite for the entire appearance: "Mr. President, they're killing

Americans!" he was able to yell above the rest. "What are you and your lame administration going to do about it?"

Once back inside the Oval Office, even the prime minister, a man who had been in and around politics for nearly forty years, could hardly believe the level of disrespect. "Did that reporter just call your administration *lame*?" he asked Dutch in astonishment. Dutch, however, smiled, placed his hand on the prime minister's back, and thanked him once again for his visit.

That level of disrespect, as noted by the Israeli Prime Minister and fueled by the fact that that reporter's question was being played over and over all morning and now late into the afternoon on the various cable news channels, wasn't lost on Gina, either, as she sat behind her desk in her small office inside the East Wing of the White House. She had a long line of meetings already scheduled by the president's staff to enhance what they called her "softer" side. This particular meeting was with members of the Society for the Prevention of Pit Bull Cruelty and she listened as they pleaded with her to get behind their cause. How supporting better treatment of pit bulls would make her appear "softer," was a mystery to her.

But even as she listened to their spiel, all she could think about was Dutch. He was adept at handling every crisis they threw his way, and could take those punches of blame, but she knew in many ways it was beginning to tear him apart. He used to joke, during the last campaign, that he didn't even want a second term. She assumed it was just the jitters and the fact that he was in a tough reelection fight. But now she wasn't so sure if it was a joke at all. She now believed, in many respects, that he sometimes hated his job.

Just like she sometimes hated hers as she sat behind her desk and listened to wealthy middle-aged ladies drone on and on about pit bulls. "When many shelters need more space," one of the women pointed out, "they will decide to euthanize pit bulls above any other breed of animal simply because of the pit bulls' reputation for violence. Forget the fact that pit bulls are no more violent than any other breed," the good lady insisted, "but they continue this practice to this day."

He made love to her for nearly two hours last night, sliding in and out of her so slowly and for so long that it intoxicated both of them: it felt like a slow-acting drug. It was so different than their usual, more aggressive sex, but it made them realize something beautiful and startling: that they had no more points to prove. They were an unshakeable couple, and they both knew it.

And then that phone call about that poor student hostage had them reeling again.

"Don't you agree, Mrs. Harber?" one of the women, Marilyn Feingold, asked.

Gina's dark brown eyes finally turned her way. "Excuse me?" she asked.

"About the death penalty for humans. It's the same thing for pit bulls. I heard you on television say that those mandatory minimum sentencing guidelines are discriminatory and I couldn't agree more."

"Yes," Gina said, now kicking herself for not paying closer attention. These ladies weren't as air-headed as she had assumed. "They are discriminatory."

"Take your brother, for instance," Feingold said. Gina wanted to quickly correct her by saying that Marcus Rance was her *half*-brother, a *half*-brother she had never even met before, but she didn't go there. He was her deceased father's son, and she wasn't sullying her own father's memory by bashing his son, no matter what Dutch's staffers insisted she do.

"What about him?" she decided to say, instead.

"He's on death row too, just like our pit bulls are. What would you tell the parole board about your brother's sentence?"

"Since I don't believe in the death penalty for anyone, including any human being like Marcus Rance or any random pit bull, I would recommend life in prison without the possibility of parole. I would be in favor of all sentences being commuted to life."

"That's how we feel about our pit bulls. They have a death sentence over their heads and nobody's advocating for their commutation to life."

"Except you guys," Gina pointed out and Marilyn Feingold couldn't help but smile.

"Yes," she said. "Except us."

Then the conversation shifted, as she compared the fate of pit bulls to unwed mothers, crack babies, and drug addicts. "To keep it real," Feingold said to Gina, as if Gina, this black woman, would have firsthand experience with all of the above.

When they finally left her office, she called Christian Bale and told him to tell Max Brennan that if his staff scheduled another meeting like that for her again, there will be blood.

Christian laughed, but then quickly called Max Brennan.

The murder of that college student created a firestorm of criticism around Dutch. Protestors, mostly partisan activists, gathered in front of the White House in the thousands, insisting that their president do something and do something now to get those poor students back home.

Dutch called an emergency meeting of his national security team. They met in the basement of the West Wing, in the vaulted Situation Room, and by the time Dutch arrived his entire national security team, from cabinet secretaries to the national security advisor and his NSC staff, were already assembled. Max, his chief of staff, was standing around with arms folded; looking nervous it seemed to Dutch, as he took his seat along the side center of the table's oval.

And it became one of the most contentious meetings they had ever had. Mainly because of the mood of the country and their desire to see results, but also because Dutch was getting sick and tired himself of their lame answers. Dutch, in fact, left the meeting early, ordering his entire team to stay where they sat until they could formulate a more definitive strategy for success and have it on his desk by eight a.m. tomorrow morning. He was slated to address the American people tomorrow night on the hostage crisis, and he wanted concrete information, not maybes and wherefores.

And then he showered and changed, hopped into an SUV, and met up with Gina and Dempsey at LaLa's home in Georgetown.

It wasn't on the manifest so the protestors didn't even realize the president had left the White House. Which they all laughed about when they turned on the TV and saw the protestors all over FOX News demanding that the president drop that same "Rose Garden Strategy" that Jimmy Carter employed, and come out and address them. "The president needs to be a man," one protestor yelled into the rolling FOX camera, "and come out of that house and answer to us."

"Turn it off," Dutch said with a chuckle as he leaned back in his chair at the head of the kitchen table and took another swig of his Guinness. Gina was seated next to him, with LaLa across from Gina and Demps at the small table's other head. Demps took the remote and turned off the television.

"What's the game plan, Mr. President?" Demps asked.

"It's currently being formulated. I don't know, Demps, sometimes I wonder if the American people are being well served by this team I selected for my administration."

"They certainly leave a lot to be desired," LaLa said and Demps gave her a *watch it* kind of harsh look.

"Don't look at me like that," she said, "I'm not taking it back. They seem like a bunch of incompetents to me. And I'm on the inside looking out."

"I agree," Gina said. "But it's too late to change course now."

Dutch glanced at his wife. She had a remarkable way of being so concise that it stopped negative energy in its tracks and moved the conversation to higher, perhaps even safer ground. She wore a sheer purple top that crisscrossed at the chest, causing him to fixate on her breasts, remembering how they taste in his mouth, and his penis began to throb in anticipation of what he knew he was going to do to her later tonight.

After dinner, an old fashioned steak and potatoes dinner that LaLa cooked and Dutch adored, they all assembled in the living room area. But they hadn't sat down ten minutes when the doorbell rang and then the door was immediately opened.

The secret service clandestinely had the outside of the home well-fortified, so it wasn't unusual for the door to be opened without permission. But when Max Brennan, rather than an agent, rounded the corner and was visible to all of them, everybody knew something was up.

"What is it now?" Dutch asked as soon as he saw his old friend's drained face.

Max placed his hands in his pant pockets as he approached. "Not good news," he said as if that needed saying.

"What is it?" Dutch asked again when he arrived at the president's side.

"They just killed Ralph Caswell," Max said and Gina, remembering Jennifer Caswell's threat, let out an audible sigh of anguish.

"Well now," Dutch said.

"There's more," Max said. "Mrs. Caswell, through her spokesman, has called a press conference for tomorrow morning. And the press is already speculating that she has plans to rake you over the coals unlike you've ever been raked before. It's as if her people have already given the press beforehand notice that she has the goods on you."

LaLa and Demps looked at Dutch. "Does she, Mr. President?" Demps asked.

Dutch and Gina exchanged glances. "Not as far as I know," Dutch said.

SIX

Dutch and Gina sat side by side in the Roosevelt Room, where the White House staff usually gathered, as the televised press conference commenced. Christian, Allison Shearer, and Max were also in the room. Gina didn't realize Dutch was holding her hand until she moved up as if she was about to get up, and he squeezed it.

The flat screen TV sat like a movie screen as they all stared unblinkingly at Jennifer. To their surprise, there was little news at the beginning of the presser, as Jennifer Caswell sounded like any other grieving widow. Until she mentioned the president's name.

"My husband saved me," she said as she stood in what appeared to be a ball room inside a hotel, the press so numerous that it was actually standing room only. "I became suicidal just after we were married. That is public knowledge. Many of my friends are aware of the fact that I was in a bad place just after I married Ralph Caswell. But what was never public knowledge was why I was in that bad place."

Max glanced at Dutch. Dutch was staring at Jennifer.

"What the public doesn't know is that I was in a long term sexual relationship with President Walter "Dutch" Harber for many years. The relationship was mutual and it was consensual. However, after I married my husband, Dutch wanted to continue the relationship and I wanted him to leave me alone so that I could be a good wife to my new husband. But he wouldn't leave me alone."

Gina could feel Dutch squeeze her hand tighter. She, too, was bracing herself.

"One night, at the White House, the President of the United States, the leader of the free world, raped me."

It felt as if a bomb had just exploded and the press didn't know what hit it. The cameras started flashing as if they were being handled by wild tabloid paparazzi, and questions started being hurled as if it was now a free-for-all. The mood became so frenzied that Jennifer's attorney, who stood alongside her, had to step in and refuse to answer any questions until the press settled back down.

The silence in the Roosevelt Room proved a startling contrast to the mayhem on the television screen. Dutch and Gina sat as if they were frozen in time, neither able to move, to speak, seemingly to breathe. Max, Allison, and Christian also stood mute. Until one of their cell phones began to rang, and then another cell phone rang, and then all three were fielding phone calls from congressmen, senators, and worried supporters about this amazing turn of events. Even LaLa and Dempsey hurried into the room, asking if they were watching Jennifer Caswell and her remarkable allegation.

Finally, the press conference was allowed to continue and one reporter, Nora Tatem, asked the obvious question. "Are you, Mrs. Caswell, accusing our sitting President of rape?"

"That's exactly what I'm accusing him of," Jennifer said, "because it's the truth. He raped me. He raped me because I would not leave my husband."

"Did you report this rape?"

"Of course not! He was the president. Nobody was going to believe me over the president!"

"Why are you coming forward now?"

"Because I believe he purposely let my husband die."

Another bombshell. Another flurry of camera flashes and numerous questions being hurled all at once. The attorney had to step in again, and then the press conference continued:

"Are you saying, Mrs. Caswell, that President Harber purposely allowed your husband to be killed by those terrorists?"

"I believe he's still so angry with me for leaving him that he did nothing to help my husband!"

"That's not the same thing, ma'am."

"It is the same thing. My husband is dead and Dutch Harber is probably sitting up in that White House gloating because of it."

"All because he still can't get over the fact that you left him for another man?"

"That's the truth. He begged me to stay with him. He still begs me."

"Are you saying the president still wants you?"

"That's what I'm saying."

"But what about the First Lady? Why would he want you, when he has her?"

Jennifer almost laughed. "The answer to that question is self-evident. Look at her, look at me, there's your answer. Next question," she said and many more questions came. But at the end of the day all of them had the same answer: Dutch Harber has committed not only a serious crime, but an impeachable offense.

And nobody in the Roosevelt Room at the White House, least of which Dutch Harber, could find the words to counter an accusation like that.

Dutch and Gina managed a little time alone later that afternoon. Dutch had been huddling with his national security team, and then his White House staff, and then his team of private lawyers, and barely managed to get away long enough to spend some time huddling with his wife.

They sat out in comfortable chairs on the Truman balcony, overlooking the South Lawn of the White House, the beauty of crabapple trees, primrose, and grape hyacinth surrounding them in stark contrast to their hectic day.

Gina looked at Dutch. He had his suit coat gaped open, his tie askew, and his hands resting on the arms of the chair, a glass of wine in one of those hands. Considering the firestorm that now swirled around him, he looked remarkably calm.

"Who were you meeting with?" she asked him.

Dutch wanted to shake his head in disgust with the fact that he had to meet with anybody at all, but didn't. "Who wasn't I meeting with might be a shorter list."

"Beyond your staff and cabinet, I mean."

"Well let me see. I've met with the White House Counsel, the Attorney General, the Secret Service, the Capitol Police, and my own private attorneys."

"The Capitol Police?" Gina asked and Dutch nodded. And it was only then did she realize he was actually near tears. "What did they want?" she asked him.

He shook his head. "They weren't sure themselves. But since the crime occurred here at the White House, and I had once been a senator, I don't know. They just heard rape and wanted in."

"Rape my eye," Gina said.

Dutch looked at her. In a lot of ways, he knew she was all he had. "Right. So she claims. Listen, Gina," he said, "I haven't had a chance to say this to you, but . . . I didn't rape that woman."

Gina frowned. "You don't have to tell me anything like that. I know you didn't rape her! Nobody's going to rape a woman like that and she not give them hell, come on. And I know rape happens and I know all kinds of women are the victims of it, I know all that. But Jennifer Caswell? That force of nature?" Gina shook her head. "I'm not buying it, sorry. Besides," she said as she touched his arm, "I know I didn't marry that kind of man."

Although Dutch was still reeling from the day's bombshell to manage any outward smile, he did smile inwardly. And thanked God Almighty for giving him a woman like Regina. "Thank-you," he said.

But then that gazed, stormy, teary-eyed look came over him again, and he looked out onto the South Lawn.

"It's just hard you know?" he said.

Gina rubbed his arm. "I know."

"The press is treating her baseless allegations as if they were gospel at a time when we're already dealing with that dangerous hostage crisis, a crisis that by its very nature is already making me seem ineffectual because I can't do a damn thing about it. Now I'm supposed to be a rapist to boot. And not just any rapist, but I supposedly raped the wife of a man who was one of the hostages, a man who was just murdered by his captors, and I supposedly raped her in the White House of all places. In the people's house."

He shook his head. "I knew they would throw the kitchen sink at me, Gina. I knew there were forces in this country who hated me, who hated my liberal policies, who hated the fact that I didn't marry a member of the elite class, although most of them aren't even members of that class themselves. But I never would have imagined that this kind of sickening charge would be thrown my way."

Then he looked at Gina with a look so pathetic, so filled with fear that it broke her heart. "How am I going to prove the negative? I didn't rape her. But how can I prove I didn't?"

"You can't prove it," Gina said. "But if you go before the American people and tell them the truth, tell them everything you know about your relationship with Jennifer, including the fact that that woman is still, to this day, in love with you, then I think they'll believe you and put this craziness to bed."

Dutch stared at her. He knew she had always been a straight shooter. "You actually believe that if I simply say it isn't so, that that will put a charge like this to rest?"

Gina exhaled, that same stormy look now crossing her tired eyes. "We have to believe it, Dutch," she said. "We have to pray and trust that God will make this entire world believe it."

Dutch stared back out at the South Lawn. "So all we have is a prayer?" he asked her.

"Sometimes, Dutch," Gina said, tears forming in her eyes, "a prayer is all we need."

Christian Bale stepped out onto the balcony. Looking his usual nervous self, Gina thought.

"Hello, Chris," she said

"Hi," he said with his ever-present smile. "Please excuse the interruption, sir, ma'am, but Mr. Bergmann and Mrs. Rice are here."

But this declaration only heightened Dutch's tension. "Can I at least have a few private moments with my wife?" he snapped. Then he calmed back down, especially when he saw Chris's face blush red. "Sorry about that, Chris. I'm just. . . Bring them out."

"Are you sure, sir? They can come back later or--"

"It's okay, Christian," Gina said. "They can come."

Christian bowed slightly and went to get the two attorneys. Peter Bergmann, the White House Counsel, and Chandra Rice, the Attorney General, crossed the Truman balcony and made their way up to the president and First Lady. Once they were offered seats, yes, and drinks, no thank-you, they got down to business.

"First of all," the Attorney General said, "there is such a thing as presidential immunity while you remain in office, although it's not completely settled law yet. But generally speaking, you should be immune from prosecution while you're in office. The proper authorities can investigate, but that's about as far as it should be able to go. Now, as to Jennifer Caswell's rape charge."

"Why is she making it?"

"Because Ralph Caswell's children, who are around the same age as Jennifer herself, plans to file a lawsuit barring her from collecting a dime of their father's billion dollar estate. She signed a pre-nup and they intend for the courts to stick to that agreement, an agreement that basically gives her little of nothing. They planned, in this lawsuit, to accuse her of basically being a gold digger, of marrying their aging father so that she could live the high life. And they say she's already squandered millions, including forcing their father to give outrageous amounts of money in her name to politicians she sleeps around with."

"She sleeps around with a lot of them?" Gina asked.

"Yes," the Attorney General said.

"And here's the kicker," Peter Bergmann, the White House counsel, said. "The Caswell siblings plan to prove that she was carrying on a torrid affair with you before and after her marriage to their father. Which we've informed the children, if they will keep silent for now, that you yourself will acknowledge in your press conference tomorrow evening. That way you'll prove their point and also prove that you didn't rape Jennifer as she claims, but that the two of you had consensual sex and you had it repeatedly."

Dutch seemed hesitant. But Gina wasn't. "Look, Dutch," she said, "by admitting such an illicit affair you won't look like a choir boy, no you won't. But at least you won't look like a rapist either."

"Right," the Attorney General agreed. "And that's why we want you on that stage beside him, Mrs. Harber. You are his most powerful weapon against the problem he has with that affair. Because if what happened before the two of you married doesn't bother you, how can it bother anybody else?"

Gina nodded her understanding. Dutch, however, disagreed. "No," he said and they all looked at him. "I will not parade my wife out in front of clicking cameras just to prove some point. What I did with Jennifer wasn't criminal, no, but it was still wrong. And I need to take that hit alone."

"Yes, you do," Gina admitted. "But this isn't about your moral lapse. This is about rape. And to prove that you didn't rape that woman I'd stand on a street corner beside you if I had to. So don't get it twisted, Dutch. I hate what you did. But I know you didn't do that other thing, and that's what my appearance will be all about. We have to fight this charge or it can ruin you forever. And that's not going to happen."

The Attorney General sighed relief. "Good," she said again. "Mrs. Caswell can't sue you while you're a sitting president, but she can certainly get the pot boiling until you leave office. That's why, yes, we want your wife on that stage beside you. To help nip this thing in the bud."

The James S. Brady press briefing room was an unlikely place to hold what many journalists were calling the press conference of the century, but Max and Allison knew what they were doing. The room was smaller than the East Room of the White House where the president normally held his pressers, which gave the feel of a pack of headline hungry journalists attacking a president already under siege. And since he was the American people's president, Max had argued, perhaps the people will themselves feel as if the press had them under siege too. Dutch personally thought it was a load of bullocks, all of this stagecraft, but he didn't argue with his chief of staff. He had enough rotten meat on his plate to argue about the gravy.

Besides, the players on the stage proved in and of itself that this was no ordinary press conference. Not only was Dutch on stage, but so was the First Lady, the White House Counsel Peter Bergmann, and Dutch's private attorney. Gina was so nervous standing there that she thought she was going to faint. Especially after Dutch gave his opening statement, which consisted of clear, blanket denials, and the questions came like shots out of cannons.

At first the questions were all about the logistics. Where, when, how. But then a shift occurred when reporter after reporter started asking, not about the president's innocence, but about whether he was going to resign or wait for Congress to draft articles of impeachment.

"*Impeachment*?" Gina said out loud before she realized she had said it, and immediately everybody in the room looked her way. She knew Max had told her to just stand there and say nothing. She knew the White House Counsel had told her to just stand there and say nothing. But *impeachment*? Where did these people get off?

"Do you believe the president's actions," a reporter quickly seized the moment and asked Gina, "warrant impeachment?"

"Of course I don't," Gina said, certain that Max and Allison Shearer, who were both standing against the side wall, were melting inside.

"Why don't you, Mrs. Harber? Your husband has been accused of rape."

Gina looked at Dutch. If he didn't want her to say what she had to say, then she'd remain silent. But Dutch, being Dutch, never cared to muzzle her. He stepped aside and allowed her to come up to the podium. Dutch glanced over at Max. If the word 'fuming' was defined in the dictionary, Max's picture would be the example underneath it.

"My concern about this talk of impeachment," Gina said, utilizing her experience as an attorney and being careful not to over speak, "is that not one word of her allegation has even been proven yet. An allegation has been made, a false allegation I might add, and you're already talking about impeachment?"

"But this is a rape charge, ma'am."

"I understand that. But it's a false rape charge."

"If you were his lawyer, Mrs. Harber," another reporter asked, "what would you advise him to do?"

Max waved his hand, as if to warn Gina against answering that tricky question, but Gina ploughed ahead anyway. "If I was advising my husband," she said, "I'd tell him what I'm telling you: to let the process take its course. If there is to be an investigation, let the authorities investigate. And then, once they find out that Mrs. Caswell's allegations are nothing more than bogus, baseless lies, then I'd advise him to have her brought up on criminal charges. And I'd also advise him to bring her up on civil charges for Defamation of Character, for starters. Especially since she lied on him while he still was a sitting president, tarnishing not only his reputation but the reputation of the entire United States of America. And then I'd sue her for those billion dollars she's trying to weasel out of his estate. She'll never see a dime of that money when we get through with her."

The press corps goes into frenzy mode as Allison yells "thank-you" and abruptly ends the press conference. Max and Peter Bergmann pretended to be in a great mood as they cleared the Brady Room, but as soon as they stepped back into the West Wing, they were livid. She just made it worse, Bergmann said.

"How's that?" Dutch wanted to know.

"Because, sir," the White House Counsel continued, "she just threatened lawsuits on a grieving widow. A grieving widow, sir. That may play well in Newark, but in middle America it looks tactless and ghetto."

Gina wanted to roll her eyes. That was always their stopgap: insult her by throwing in the word ghetto at every turn. And she started to tell him about his nature self, but Dutch beat her to it.

"You may wish to coddle Jennifer Caswell," he said, "but since she's accused me of raping her, my wife and I have decided against that strategy. And everything my wife said in that briefing room is exactly what needed to be said. And it's the truth. I will sue her pants off if she continues with this charade. We're playing hardball gentlemen, from here on out, so don't try to make my wife the villain. That blonde-haired, blue-eyed devil you're trying to coddle is the villain here. And don't you forget it. And Peter," Dutch added as he and Gina were about to leave, "if you ever attempt to disparage my wife again by referencing the 'ghetto,' I will get 'ghetto' myself and publicly humiliate your ass. Understand me?"

"Yes, sir," Bergmann said nervously. "Sir, I didn't mean---"

"Yes, you did, you meant it. So don't even try to front," Dutch said and then he and Gina walked away.

Only Gina walked away smiling. *"Don't even try to front?"* she said incredulously to her husband.

"I've heard you use it beautifully," he said, smiling too. "So why can't I use it too? Even if I don't quite know what it means."

They both broke into laughter. Max and Bergmann just stood there, in the West Wing corridor, wondering what in the world, at a time like this, could possibly be so funny.

Later that night, Gina lay on top of Dutch, her head on his bare chest, his penis sliding in and out of her naked ass. His arms were tight around her as he fucked her, as their eyes were closed to the realities of the day. That was why, when the secure phone rang, Dutch was almost hesitant to answer it.

But of course he did.

When he hung up, Gina's head was off of his chest, and her worried eyes were staring down at him.

"That was Max," he said, more of a shocked look in his eyes. "Jennifer Caswell will issue a statement saying that she is withdrawing all charges against me."

Gina sat up on top of Dutch, amazed. "Are you serious?"

"Yes. According to this statement of hers, she will say that she was in shock following her beloved husband's death and she therefore wanted to blame me and consequently misspoke."

"She misspoke? She calls accusing a sitting president of rape misspeaking?"

Dutch nodded, amazed too. Then he looked at Gina. "Before she will issue the statement, however, she wants assurances that I will agree not to pursue any law suits against her."

Gina smiled.

"Seems your threats at that press conference tonight had a profound effect on the good lady."

"Good lady my ass," Gina said. "One of the first things I've learned in this life, Dutch, is that money talks. The fact that we threatened to take away any money she may or may not receive from that man's estate is what's driving her sudden change of heart. Believe that."

Dutch stared at his wife, admiring her even more. "Well believe this," he said, pulling her back into his arms, his dormant penis reasserting itself inside of her. "I love you dearly. Even though you can be a pain in the ass sometimes," he added with a grin.

"Oh yeah?" she said as his penis began to increase in its fluidity. "Bet I'm no ass pain now."

And Dutch, realizing what she meant, couldn't help but laugh.

SEVEN

After the Jennifer Caswell story left the headlines as quickly as it had appeared, the hostage crisis, although still front page news, began to lose its intensity too. Mainly because there was no new news, no more proof of life videos, no new demands or threats from the captors. But also because of the behind the scenes maneuvering by SEALS teams that the press was alerted by the White House to not report for security reasons. But within a week of this more peaceful madness, a new story broke, this one so ridiculous on its face that not even the president's chief of staff saw it coming.

It was after the president and the Speaker of the House had played eighteen rounds of golf at the usual secluded location inside Andrews Air Force Base. Max and the Vice President were also in attendance as they prepared to leave the base known for shuttling heads of state in and out of the country, when Max reminded the president that the press was also waiting.

Although Dutch hated photo-ops in general, he knew he and the Speaker were required to stand before the press and give them one. And they did. They smiled, shook hands, joked about both being winners, and prepared to walk away. Questions were being hurled, as they always were when the president was in earshot, until one caught his ear and couldn't be ignored.

"Why did the First Lady intervene to help Marcus Rance, sir?" the reporter asked.

Dutch and Max stopped in their tracks, causing the others to stop too. Dutch glanced at Max. Max shrugged. Then Dutch walked back toward the press corps. As soon as he did, the reporter clarified his question.

"Your wife's brother, sir, has had his death sentence commuted to life after your wife intervened on his behalf. My question to you is, sir, why would she do such a thing, given his heinous crimes, and isn't it a conflict of interest for her to have done so?"

"My wife," Dutch said, careful not to lose his cool, "did not intervene in any way on behalf of her *half*-brother, a brother she has never even met, or anyone else. I don't know who fed you that story, but they fed you a load of garbage."

And then Dutch walked away, with Max, the Vice President, and the Speaker of the House, hurrying behind him.

But Dutch wasn't back inside the West Wing an hour before Max and Allison were coming into the Oval Office with more information.

"It's true, sir," Max said as soon as he walked up to his desk.

Dutch was seated behind his desk, his reading glasses on, as he and the National Security Advisor reviewed, for the tenth time, the hostage rescue and its operational progress. Dutch looked up at Max, frowning.

"What's true?" he wanted to know.

"She did intervene on behalf of Marcus Rance."

Dutch removed his glasses and leaned back in his chair. "That'll be all, Eddie," he said to his National Security Advisor.

Ed Drake, understanding, quickly left the office.

"What the hell are you talking about, Max?"

Max sat down in front of the desk. Allison remained standing. "It's even in the White House guest log, Dutch."

"What's in the guest log?"

"The fact that Gina met with Marilyn Feingold, the wife of the governor of Texas, and that even Mrs. Feingold is admitting that Gina attempted to intervene. Feingold, of course, declares Gina's intervention had nothing to do with her husband's ultimate decision to accept the defense request and commute Marcus Rance's death sentence to life in prison without the possibility of parole. She declares that the facts of the case are what influenced his decision. But it just stinks like mad, Dutch."

Dutch remained calm, although he was raging inside. "And why would the governor want to help my supposed brother-in-law?"

"Because he chaired the Texas branch of your reelection campaign, remember?" Allison said. "He'll be out as governor next year and he's been angling for a cabinet post in your administration after his term is over."

"And he thought," Dutch said, his temper rising, "that he could gain my support by commuting the sentence of some murderer? Just because that murderer happens to be my wife's half-brother?"

Allison looked at Max.

"Yes, sir," Max said disgustedly too. "That's exactly what that fool thought."

Gina sat in the master dressing room within the second floor residence, on the southwest corner of the White House, and looked at the rack of designer gowns at her disposal. LaLa was in the room with her, and so were three other assistants, as she attempted to find the perfect gown for the upcoming state dinner. It was a relaxed, festive environment, until the president walked in.

The aides, who were perfectly relaxed with Gina, became stiff and formal on his arrival.

"Hello, sir," LaLa said with a smile. "Please tell your wife that another McQueen gown won't cut it. She needs to expand her horizons a little more. Trying something daring."

Dutch stood over Gina, looking at the rack of clothes. "Which one is your preference?" he asked his wife.

"This one," she said, pointing to a McQueen gown of lace and careful stitching.

"It's gorgeous," Dutch said, and Gina smiled.

"Two to one in favor," Gina said to her friend. "So much for your daring," she added.

"Whatever," LaLa said with a smile.

Dutch, however, placed his hands in his pocket and walked toward the window. When he did that, Gina looked at LaLa.

"Okay, girls," LaLa said as she began to leave, "let's go and do some real work, shall we?"

LaLa and the aides left. When they did, Gina walked over to Dutch and they both stared out of the window.

"What is it?" she asked him.

"Your meeting with Marilyn Feingold," he said.

Gina frowned. "Who?"

"Marilyn Feingold," Dutch said, looking at her. "The wife of the governor of Texas. You know Texas? Where your brother is serving his prison time?"

Gina didn't like his snide tone. "If you're asking if I remember meeting with her, the answer is yes. But she never said she was the governor's wife. I just thought she was a member of some organizations. She may have assumed I knew who she was, but I didn't. It wasn't until she had left did one of my aides point out that she was the wife of the governor of Texas."

"But you discussed Marcus Rance with her?"

"No, not really."

"What does that mean, Gina? Either you discussed him or you didn't!"

"What are you jumping down my throat for?"

"Did you discuss him?"

Gina was suddenly concerned by Dutch's harsh tone. What had she done now? "We talked, yes, and she did mention the death penalty, and she gave an example and we discussed it."

"What example?"

"She was talking about pit bulls."

Dutch frowned. "Pit bulls?"

"That's why she was here. She and some other ladies represented the Society for the Prevention of Cruelty to Pit Bulls or some such name."

"Who the hell would have scheduled a meeting like that for you?"

"Somebody on Max's team actually," Gina said. "I did voice my displeasure."

"What did this Society want with you?"

Gina smiled. "They wanted me to take up the cause of pit bull cruelty, can you believe it? I mean, I don't want to see pit bulls brutalized, and I understand the problems they face, but come on? There are crack babies out there, babies born with AIDs, hungry families, people losing their homes, and they want me to invest the little good will I do have with the American people on pit bull cruelty? Apparently the woman who had set it up has a pit bull herself and she thought it would be a neat cause."

Dutch shook his head. "Next time they schedule meetings like that for you, you tell me about it."

"I will."

"But what about Marcus Rance? Did his name come up?"

"It came up, yes, that's what I was saying. Mrs. Feingold bought it up herself, comparing the plight of pit bulls to the plight of people on death row. She knew I opposed capital punishment of any kind. And she asked if I would want my brother's sentence commuted to life."

Dutch closed his eyes as soon as she said that, and then reopened them. "And of course you said you would?"

"I said I was against the death penalty for any reason and for anybody, so yes, I said I would. Not because of my kinship with Marcus Rance, such as it is, but because of the principal of capital punishment itself. That was it, Dutch, I declare that was it." Then she stared at his troubled eyes. "Why?"

"Oh, nothing, except that Marcus Rance's sentence has just been commuted to life by Mrs. Feingold's husband. Thanks, according to the press, to your intervention."

Gina couldn't believe it. She just stood there staring at Dutch.

Dutch exhaled. "Damn," he said.

"But it was nothing!" Gina insisted. "It was just an offhand comment."

"Gina, how many times do I have to tell you to watch what you say around here, offhand or not?" Dutch exhaled, ran his hand through his thick mop of black hair. "It was no issue, you know it and I know it. But the press, they don't know that. Little offhand comments like this are their bread and butter, and don't you forget that!"

Gina stared at Dutch. Her *fed-up with this town* meter was slowly moving off the charts. "What can I do?" she asked in a deflated tone, because she knew there was always some sick, political, pandering way to make it up.

"Max suggests you go to one of those victims of violent crime centers here in DC and meet with some of the victims. That way you'll look more sympathetic to the victims rather than the perps."

"I am sympathetic to the victims."

"You know it, I know it. We need to make sure the public still knows it."

Gina shook her head. "But to have me going to a victim center after the commutation, like the American people are stupid or something. That is so bogus, Dutch."

"I know it is. But do it," he ordered, looking her dead in the eye.

Gina nodded, still reluctant. "Yes, sir," she said.

Dutch kissed her lightly on the lips, and left.

"Shoes," Gina said aloud, and went back to her rack of gowns.

Two days later, after visiting two of those victim centers in the DC area and actually learning something she thought was rather profound, she made a decision. That night, alone in the residence with Dutch, she tried to figure out a way to tell him about it.

"How did it go today?" she asked him. They were in the residence dining hall eating dinner. Dutch at the head of the table, Gina sitting to the right of him.

"It was the usual unusual, you know how it goes. Plans are being drawn and redrawn, the economy is beginning to pick up some steam, and we're finally having some private communications with the hostage takers."

"The media would broadcast it live if they found out."

"Some already know. The big three networks know, but for the safety of the hostages they have agreed to keep it under wraps."

"Really? And you expect them to keep their word?"

"It's happened before. As long as they know the hostages' lives are at stake, they'll remain silent."

"I pray you're right."

"Also," Dutch said a little less enthusiastically. "My mother phoned."

Gina bit into a biscuit and looked at him. "What did she want?"

"To see me."

Not us, Gina thought. "Where?"

"Nantucket."

"Are you going?"

Dutch hesitated, staring down at his bowl of soup. "Yes," he said. "I'm still upset with her for opposing our marriage, and doing so publicly, but she's still my mother." Gina nodded. "And she says it's very important that she sees me."

"What could be so important?"

"I don't know. But I'm assuming it's personal."

"You mean she could be ill or something?"

"She's sixty-four years old. It's possible."

Gina nodded. Then she told him about her day at those victim centers and what happened during her last few minutes at one of them.

"I was just giving my usual spiel, you know," she said, "about how things will get better and how to look on the bright side and I stayed away from all controversy and focused only on sunshine and happiness. Max would have been proud. I even told a group of teenage victims to forgive their perpetrators, saying that not forgiving only hurts them."

"You told them right," Dutch said, reaching for another biscuit to dip into the wonderful pea soup the Chef had prepared.

"I know it was the right thing to say," Gina replied. "But then one of them, a real skinny kid with little squinty eyes, asked if I had forgiven my brother."

Dutch looked at her. "Forgiven him?"

"Yeah. For being a drug dealer. For that drive-by he committed and those people died. For disgracing my father's name. He wanted to know if I forgave him for that."

"What did you say?"

"I told the truth. I said no. I mean, I haven't even thought about Marcus Rance, at least not like that. But then the kid says, 'how can you ask us to forgive, when you can't even do it?' That just stunned me, Dutch. Not only was I a fake for even agreeing to go to that center to begin with, just to appease some press that won't give us credit anyway, but I was being a hypocrite about it too."

"You're being too hard on yourself."

Gina hesitated. Then stared at her husband. "I want to see him, Dutch."

Dutch could hardly believe his ears. "See him? Why?"

"Because he's my father's son. Because I need to look him in the eye and I don't know why. But I want to go and see him. I just think I should see him. He is my brother."

"He's your half-brother."

"He's my father's whole son, Dutch. And I loved my father. I feel I should do this."

Dutch was shaking his head before she finished her sentence. "That's out of the question, Regina," he said.

"But why?"

"What do you mean why? The mid-terms are coming up."

"Not for another two years."

"But people don't forget. We've got to elect more Democrats. I don't need a Republican House that I'll have to fight tooth and nail in the last years of my term. But that's exactly what will happen if I keep making a mess of things for our party. And if I let you go to some prison in Texas to see that man, it'll be the very definition of making a mess of things."

"But I need to see him, Dutch."

"Because some kid asked you a question? Come on, Gina!"

"Because I need to see him. He's my flesh and blood."

"He's a murderer."

"He's my brother who happens to be a murderer. I understand he's a terrible, despicable human being. But that doesn't change the fact that he's my flesh and blood and I think I should go and see him."

"No."

"Oh, so you can go and see your racist mother but I can't go and see my brother?"

"Half-brother. And it's not the same thing."

"Why isn't it?"

"Because my mother didn't kill anyone! My mother wasn't on death row!"

"And your mother," Gina said, "isn't always at the center of political controversies that hurts the Democratic Party."

Dutch looked at Gina, threw his napkin onto the table, and stood and left.

Gina threw her napkin onto the table too. But she just sat there.

A day later, Dutch took Air Force One out of Andrews Air Force Base and then Marine One to his mother's estate on Nantucket Island, leaving from the guest room before Gina woke up. And Gina, once awake, took a Boeing 757 out of Andrews and then a convoy of SUVs to the Alan B. Polunsky Unit of the Texas State Penitentiary in West Livingston, Texas.

EIGHT

Dutch sat in the parlor of his mother's home, his muscular body leaned forward, his arms resting on his thighs as he read a series of text messages on his customized, Secret Service-issued Blackberry. Although he was reading the messages, he couldn't stop thinking about Gina and that awful argument they had had last night. Then to get word from a member of his staff, while he was en route here to Nantucket, that she had decided to go to Livingston anyway, concerned him.

Just after their marriage, when parts of America was stunned, other parts elated, the Secret Service chief had asked if Dutch wanted to have final approval over all of the First Lady's travel itinerary. Dutch had thought it rather condescending for him to even ask it, as if he expected Gina to hop a plane to rendezvous with one of her lovers or something, and he had said no without hesitation. And even now he stood by his decision. Gina was too smart and savvy a lady for him to dream of keeping tabs on her, and he told that chief, who seemed to be among those more stunned than elated by the marriage, that his wife was more than capable of approving her own schedules.

But he still worried about her. She wanted to meet this half-brother of hers, this murderer Marcus Rance, when Dutch knew that going down a road like that rarely, if ever, ended well. Although he did understand her curiosity. This Rance fellow was, as she rightly pointed out, the only son of her beloved, deceased father. But he also was a cold, calculating killer who decided to do a drive-by that mowed down those innocent people as if they were targets on a shooting range. And he didn't want a guy like that playing with his wife's emotions. Because Dutch knew that Gina was an advocate to her soul, a woman who never met a human being she viewed as beyond redemption. And his fear was that she'd go down there to Texas, find in this brother of hers another redemption project, and begin advocating for him. Which could be painful for her. Not to mention, as Max did repeatedly on their ride over, politically devastating for him.

But Marcus Rance was her blood relative, and Dutch understood her need to connect. But even so it had been Dutch's experience, with his own mother as his guide, that some blood relatives, when those layers peeled away, were better left alone.

Max, who was with Dutch and sat beside him on the sofa, could not have agreed more and told the president so on their ride over to Massachusetts. But it went in one ear and out the next, it seemed to Max, because the president, for all of his great skills of human acumen, was tone-deaf when it came to that wife of his. She could parade around Washington in her Dashikis and braids and the rest of that African shit she loved to wear, could cuss out reporters, could behave like the ghetto-fabulous hood rat she really was, and he just sat back and let

113

her. Slap the shit out of her was what he needed to do, Max figured, but could he tell that to Dutch? To his best friend since they were kids together on this very island? Not if he wanted to keep his job. Not if he wanted to keep his teeth. Not if he wanted to keep his life!

And now this phone call from Victoria. What was this about? What, he wondered as he sat there, could possibly be this important that a proud lady like Dutch's mother, who had vowed to never speak to her son again after his marriage to Gina, would have insisted that he come?

But before Max could even propose the question to Dutch, the doors were opened by longtime household servant Nathan Riles, and Victoria Harber, along with another petite woman, walked in. As soon as Max saw the woman walking in behind Victoria, he stood, in utter shock, to his feet.

"Hello, Maxwell," Victoria said, pleased by his reaction.

Max, however, couldn't speak.

Victoria smiled and looked beyond Max. "Hello, Walter."

Dutch stopped reading his text messages as he slowly looked up. When he saw his mother, he stood up, slipping his Blackberry inside his coat lapel. "Hello, Mother," he said as he began to approach her, his eyes scanning the length of her as if to determine, in a cursory way, if this request for him to come had anything to do with her health. Which, he concluded, given her upbeat appearance, it did not.

But when his eyes moved from his mother and landed on the younger woman now beside her, a sudden sense of déjà vu hit him, and then the reality of it hit just as hard, and he stopped in his tracks.

It had to be a mirage, a trick of the eyes, a harsh, cruel hoax.

"Yes," his mother said, smiling greatly now. "It's Caroline!"

Dutch just stood there, staring at the younger woman. Max moved up beside him, staring too.

"But," Max said in a voice so shocked it sounded like an exhale. "How can this be?"

Dutch, however, still just couldn't believe it. Caroline? The woman he had planned to marry, was ready to marry, had made all of the arrangements to marry? Or did she just favor her? That had to be it. Perhaps she was just an older version of the woman he used to love so completely. Because it couldn't be. It just *couldn't*. Caroline died in that plane crash over a dozen years ago. How could she be standing here today?

Victoria, seeing her son's distress, touched Caroline on the arm. Caroline, more affected by seeing Dutch again than she thought she would be, began to move toward him. He was older now, but he was the same too. He was still so gorgeous, still so virile, still that same man who used to wrap her too tightly in his arms; who used to make love to her in such a way that no man, not even her beloved Pierre, had ever been able to match.

When he became president, she had thought to reassert herself in his life then. But it would mean telling Pierre about her sordid past. And she wasn't about to do that. Besides, her life was idyllic then. She had a rich, fantastic looking, just as virile husband, lived in the perfect French villa, had all those other fantastic-looking, virile Frenchmen clandestinely at her disposal. Until the French authorities came, arrested Pierre for running what they said was an international Ponzi scheme that financially crippled thousands of unsuspecting investors, and she was left devastated, poverty-stricken, and alone.

Now her savior was in front of her, the man she was determined to reclaim. Twelve years ago, Victoria Harber was the only one who could ruin her, because she was the only one with the evidence. Others in their circle suspected Caroline of infidelity, of sleeping around with every Tom, Dick, and Harry, but Victoria was the only one with the video to prove that Caroline was nothing more than a high-class slut of a nymphomaniac. And she warned her: if she showed up at that altar, she would expose her for what she truly was right there in that church. Dutch would dump her, their circle would abandon her, and she'd be left penniless and alone.

The plan, as hatched by Victoria and agreed by Caroline, was that Caroline would go to France on the pretense of finalizing the arrangements on the villa where she and Dutch planned to stay on their honeymoon. She would fly over on one of the

Harber's private jets, tell the pilot at the last minute to leave without her, and then she'd keep the money Victoria had given to her, some half a million dollars, and get lost in that vast French countryside. But then, as if fate itself intervened, the plane that left without her did what planes sometimes were prone to do and crashed. Giving her an out, an airtight reason why she was not coming back to Dutch: the plane crashed into the mountains, leaving no survivors. And she was therefore counted among those dead bodies that ended up scattered like incinerated ashes along the northern face of Mont Pelvoux, in the picturesque French Alps.

And suddenly an improbable life, where she could change her identity, live off of Victoria's half million until she could meet and marry one of those rich Frenchmen whom she just knew would go goo-goo eyed over a beauty like her, became possible.

But after Pierre's arrest and her eviction from their villa, all their money and possessions seized by authorities, and with nowhere else to turn: she turned to Victoria. And now Victoria was on her side. Not because she suddenly loved her and was so thrilled she didn't die in that plane crash that she wanted to welcome her back with open arms. But because, in Regina Lansing, Victoria had finally found a woman even more ill-suited for her special son.

Dutch, however, didn't have the advantage of all of that back story. All he knew was what he saw in front of him. And all he saw was that the woman he once loved with all of his heart, the woman he thought was long since dead, appeared to be standing right in front of him. Still petite, still had that long, healthy, shiny black hair, still had those undeniably sexy hazel eyes.

"Caroline?" Dutch said as if it were an impossible question to even ask. Because intellectually he knew it couldn't be. But emotionally he knew, somehow he was certain, that it was.

"Hello, Dutch," Caroline said as age lines appeared on the sides of her gorgeous eyes. She was twenty-five at that time of that plane crash, and Dutch had just turned thirty-two. She would be thirty-eight years old now. And although she still looked remarkably beautiful, she also looked every year of her age. Whatever journey she had traveled, Dutch decided, it hadn't been an easy road.

"I know you're shocked," Caroline continued. "But I assure you it's me."

"But it can't be," Max said, still reeling too. "You died in that plane crash. In the Alps for crying out loud! Are you telling us there was no plane crash? That those people didn't die?"

"They died. And I was listed on the flight itinerary. But I wasn't on that plane. I thank God I wasn't, considering the tragedy that occurred, but as fate would have it, I had decided to stay in France."

Dutch stared at her. Caroline immediately felt that same discomfort she used to feel when he would seem to be studying her so intensely. "Why?" he asked her.

She and Victoria had rehearsed this moment. She was never to mention the fact that Victoria, before the crash, had paid her to stay, had threatened to expose her "problem" if she so much as thought about coming back. The plane crash was incidental, a fluke of nature that took care of all questions back then. Dutch would simply believe she was lost forever, like the rest of those poor souls, in the crash. But now, when questions needed answering, when Victoria had told her exactly what to say, words failed her. It was that earnest look in his deep green eyes that spooked her.

Tears came. And to her surprise and certainly to Victoria's, she couldn't staunch the flow.

When she began to cry, Dutch remembered her. He remembered her so vividly that it stunned him. And he pulled her into his arms.

Victoria pressed her hand to her chest as Dutch held Caroline. There wasn't an actress in Hollywood that could have put on a better performance. No words, no histrionics, just simple tears. And just like that, Victoria thought with great cheer, Caroline Parker belonged to Dutch again. And the Harber family gene pool was safe.

They allowed the First Lady to wait in the Warden's office. This was so unprecedented that they didn't know what else to do. No one of her caliber had ever come to Polunsky to see a prisoner before. To see the prison, yes, the high and mighties loved to tour the facilities and accidentally see a random prisoner or two. But none of this caliber had ever had a specific inmate in mind.

Gina leaned back in the big, uncomfortable executive chair behind the Warden's oversized desk. Christian was with her and was so protective that he stood beside her chair the entire time. LaLa was there too, sitting in front of the desk, but she hated prisons and was as muted as the secret service agents in the room.

When Gina realized that Christian was literally hovering over her, she smiled and told him to sit down.

"I can't do that, ma'am," he said. "The president expects me to protect you."

Gina smiled. Christian was like a son to Dutch, but Dutch was like some great, mythical figure to Christian. His every move seemed to center around making sure he was doing right by Dutch.

Dutch, Gina thought, as her mind drifted to their dust-up last night. It was their first severe argument and it was a doosie. It was so bad that Dutch not only walked out on her, but he spent the night in the guest room. And it wasn't because he had a late meeting, either. It was because he had had it with her.

He was opposed to what she was about to do, and she understood his concern. But what hurt her was the way he never once tried to see it from her point of view. Yes, Marcus Rance was the scum of the earth for the crimes he was convicted of committing. Gina was one of those attorneys who had seen it all and she knew all about those drive-by shootings where the shooter had such low regard for life that he didn't care who was caught in the crossfire. He knew Marcus's crimes were inexcusable.

But he was still her father's son. He was still her flesh and blood. And now that he was off Death Row and granted permission to have guests, she felt compelled to come.

The timing was wrong, she understood that. Dutch's political opponents and what Sarah Palin rightly called that *lame street* beltway media would try to make hay out of it, she knew that too. But ever since she found out about Marcus Rance's existence last year, she'd wanted to see him. But it was an impossibility then. Dutch was in a bitter re-election campaign and the press was trying, through her, to link him in every way to Marcus Rance. No way was she going to give them the hammer to hammer Dutch with.

But the election was over now and Dutch had won. He was now constitutionally barred from ever seeking the presidency again and therefore, for all intents and purposes, his political campaigns were over. The Democratic Party was relying on his support, of course, but that, Gina felt, wasn't about her. She wasn't delaying any longer seeing her father's son because of any allegiance she had to the Democratic Party.

And when Marcus Rance walked into the Warden's office, chained from hand to foot like the animal he probably was, surrounded by not only prison guards, but the Secret Service too, Gina understood Dutch's resistance. Because in just that moment she was resistant too. She wanted to get up and run away herself.

But she didn't. She stayed. And what struck her was the familiarity of him. In the newspaper photos of him, which were always mug shots, he looked like some wild-haired, menacing-looking thug of a man. But now, in person, he was this short, chubby, bespectacled, nerdy-looking man who looked remarkably, almost uncannily, like her father.

"Sit down, Rance," the Warden ordered as guards pressed on his shoulders and slammed him down into the chair in front of the desk. After Gina assured the Warden that she was fine, he and the guards left. The Secret Service, however, remained in the background, but they remained.

"I know who you are," Rance said with a wide, gap-tooth grin.

"Oh, yeah?"

"Yes ma'am. You're my sister. Oh, and the First Lady of course."

"And you're Marcus Rance, my father's son, the convicted murderer of innocent people."

Rance's grin left. He glanced at the Secret Service, at Christian, and then he looked more suspiciously at Gina. "What's all this about?" he asked.

"I wanted to meet you. I wanted to see how you could come from a great, wonderful man like my father, and do the things you did."

"Great and wonderful?" Rance said incredulously. "When was he so great and wonderful? Before or after he left my mama while she was pregnant with me? Before or after she had to take him to court just to get a little child support, and even then he denied paternity? Before or after my mama died and those state social workers tried to get him to come and get me and he wouldn't. And I was put in foster home after foster home where I was beaten, falsely accused, and raped so many times that I wanted to kill the next motherfucker who so much as looked at me funny. But of course our daddy had nothing to do with all of that. He was too busy being great and wonderful."

He exhaled. Looked her up and down. "Try living with those kind of odds stacked against you, *sis*, and I'd bet what side of that desk you would have been on today! No rich, white president would have wanted to fuck you then!"

The secret service quickly moved for Rance but Gina stopped them. She was shaken by his harsh past and by her father's part in that harshness, but she willed herself not to show it.

When the agents backed off, she looked Rance dead in the eye. "Are you saying that, in light of your background, your behavior should be excused?"

"That's what you saying. I'm not saying that. I know I messed the fuck up. I know I did some stupid shit in my day. But the crime they're accusing me of, I didn't do."

Gina smiled. "Oh. You're innocent. I see."

"I didn't say anything about being innocent. I'm not innocent. But I didn't do no drive-by and kill those people, I'm saying that. Because it's the truth."

Gina stared at her brother.

"Why you think they commuted my sentence?" he asked. "Because they know it too. Look at the evidence, if you don't believe me."

"What will I find if I look?"

Rance seemed to move to the edge of his seat, prompting an agent to move closer to him. He glanced at that agent, bitterly, but then looked at Gina. "You'll find that I was at work when they said that drive-by happened."

"Work?" Gina blurted out. "What work? According to press accounts you were a drug dealer when that crime occurred."

"But that ain't the truth. Yeah, okay, I slung drugs when I was a kid, but I been out of that. I was working all kinds of jobs since then. I was working at Winchell's when that drive-by happened. Had clocked in and everything. And made my rounds like I always do."

"What's Winchell's? And what kind of rounds were you making?"

"Winchell's is a furniture store in Abilene. I deliver furniture, that's what rounds I make. And I was delivering furniture when they said that drive-by occurred."

"Are they saying you shot those people in your delivery truck?"

"No! They say I shot them in my car, and that car been stolen for like two weeks."

Christian almost smiled. That story was absurd to even him. But Gina and even LaLa, to his surprise, didn't seem to find it absurd at all.

"Did you report your car as stolen?"

"Yeah I reported it! But them police trying to say they don't have no record of it."

"And did your employer testify that you were at work?"

"He testified. Said I clocked in. Then them prosecutors twisted him all up till he said he couldn't verify for sure that I stayed on my delivery route the whole time, even though the family I delivered the furniture to said I got there at the time I was supposed to get there."

"So they believe while on your way to that delivery you went and committed yourself a drive-by shooting?"

"That's what they saying. But I would have had to ditch the truck, take my partner with me--"

"What partner?"

"The employee who delivered furniture with me," Rance said, amazed that she didn't know every detail of his case. "His name's Jason Craig. But because he ain't upstanding either they didn't believe his report at all." Then Rance looked Gina dead in the eye. "There are so many holes in this conviction, sis, you wouldn't believe it. And they convicted me anyway. It was like my past was on trial, not my present, not my future, not whether or not I did what they said I did. It was terrible."

Gina could see the horror in his eyes, as if he was still amazed himself by what he perceived to be a monumental miscarriage of justice. And she didn't' dismiss his claim out of hand because she couldn't; because in her nearly decade work with Block by Block Raiders in Newark, she'd seen even worse.

"What's your lawyer's name?" she asked the man whom she still couldn't reconcile as her brother.

NINE

Victoria and Max stood at the lunette window and watched as Dutch and Caroline walked in deliberately slow strides across the Nantucket estate. It reminded both of them of the old days, when the pair was so much in love that it was ridiculous to Max even then. At least Dutch was deeply in love. Max had already discovered and Victoria eventually found out, that Caroline loved Dutch, but so many other men, too.

"They make a very loving couple," Victoria said, as if the past was nothing more than a truth to be forgotten.

Max looked at her, and then back at the couple. He couldn't forget that easily. "An attractive one, in any event."

Victoria, however, scoffed at his insinuation. "She looks better with him than that Regina person any day of the week, I assure you of that."

Max looked at Victoria. "You don't like Gina?"

"Do you, Maxwell?"

Max shrugged his shoulders. "She's growing on me, how's that?"

Victoria snorted. "You don't like her, either."

"I didn't say that, Vicky. She's been an overall asset to Dutch. I mean, she loves the guy and the guy loves her. Besides, it was her quick thinking and legal smarts that saved his bacon at that press conference last week."

"What save? She threatened Jennifer Caswell with a lawsuit, something ambulance-chasing lawyers like her are great at doing: Tossing threats. But as the First Lady tossing these threats around? Oh, come now, Max. It's ludicrous to even consider." She stared at the twosome on the estate grounds. "But then there's Caroline," she said. "And although I have my issues with her, yes, I do, she's still head and shoulders above that hood rat."

Max looked back out of the window too, as Caroline carefully slid her arm through Dutch's. That chick, with Victoria as her mentor, knew exactly what she was doing. "You do understand," Max said, "that Caroline herself is half-black?"

Victoria continued to look out of the window. "I know that there were once rumors to that effect, vicious rumors that her biological mother was black--"

"It's no rumor, Vicky," Max pointed out, "it's a fact. Your husband, God rest his soul, had his people investigate it. I led that investigation. She was adopted by white parents, she was raised as a white girl, but her biological mother, the woman whose circumstances forced her to give that child up for adoption, was a black woman."

"Be that as it may," Victoria said, "but at least it's well hidden. At least Caroline, unlike that Regina person, doesn't flaunt her blackness."

Max looked at Victoria. How in the world did Gina "flaunt" her blackness? By being black? By living as a black? Or maybe she just felt like he did that Gina could at least tone it down a bit. But then again, unlike Max, Victoria Harber was supposed to understand these things. She was a champion of blacks everywhere after all, a liberal icon. Max inwardly smiled. That was Victoria Harber for you: a woman who would give until it hurt to the poor, while all the while hating them for the very fact that they were poor.

"I need you on this, Maxwell," Victoria said as she and Max looked at each other. "I know about your political ambitions. Yes, I know about that."

Max was astounded. "I haven't announced anything. I haven't told anyone--"

"You were making the kinds of inquiries that take no rocket scientist to figure out. My spies figured it out. And even Walter doesn't know, I'm aware of that too. But I know. I have connections you wouldn't believe. Money gets you everything these days. And with that money I could financially assist those ambitions of yours. I could make your dreams come true." Max turned toward her. She almost smiled at his eagerness. "But my money and my support doesn't come free, Maxwell. There will be times when you will have to assist me too." She looked him dead in the eye. "Understand?"

Making a deal with her was like dealing with the devil, but he nodded anyway. And looked back out of the window, at the president and his lady.

Caroline Parker aimed to worm her way back into the president's life: there was no doubt in Max's mind about that now. Her goal, aided and abetted by the president's mother herself, was to use the sentiment of their past love to steal Dutch from Gina. What was surprising to Max, however, was that Dutch looked like a man so caught up in the grips of that past sentiment, so stunned that his first true love was back within his grasp, that he just might not mind being stolen.

The twosome sat on a bench in front of the lake, as Dutch crossed his legs and Caroline snuggled further into her thick sweater. A smattering of secret service agents, some visible, many not, blanketed the estate.

"Cold?" Dutch asked, knowing that he would be a poor judge of the weather right now. The shock of seeing her again still had him reeling, still made him feel almost infernal.

"A bit, yes," Caroline said.

Dutch immediately removed his suit coat and placed it over her small, delicate shoulders. He remembered those shoulders; remembered kissing them and caressing them; remembered feeling so protective of them.

"Now you're cold," she said in her sweet, coquettish way.

"No, I'm fine," Dutch said truthfully. "Cold is the least that I am."

Caroline looked at him. "Still shocked?"

Dutch nodded. "That would be an understatement."

"I know, babe." Dutch looked at her. She used to always call him babe. "I just didn't know where to turn. Talk about shock. That's what I was in. My husband had really done a number on me."

"Was it another woman?"

"No! He was very faithful. In some ways, I wish it was as simple as another woman."

"Tell me what happened to you, Caroline." Dutch said this with pain in his voice. "Why did you let me believe you were dead?"

"I was supposed to go to France to make sure everything would be ready for our honeymoon. That was the purpose of the trip; that was why your mother had arranged it." Caroline looked away from Dutch when she told this lie: his mother had arranged for her to go to France, all right. But not to prepare for their honeymoon, as both she and Victoria were telling others, but for her to take up permanent residence at a Villa in Provence, France, where she would remain with five hundred thousand dollars cash from the Harber estate. If she resurfaced in any way, shape or form, those sex tapes, and there were many, would be shown to Dutch and the world, and she'd be castigated even worse.

But she wasn't about to tell Dutch any of that.

"I felt as if I was under so much pressure," she went on, "that I just kind of had a breakdown. I couldn't come back."

"So you stayed in France?"

"I stayed. I just stayed. The plane was leaving, and I was on the flight manifest, but I told the pilot to leave without me, that you had decided that I would stay for a few days longer. He didn't question it, he just did what I instructed him to do and he and his crew left. I never dreamed there would be an accident." Tears welled up in her eyes. "I never dreamed that that poor man and his crew would be killed. But, as life sometimes would have it, it became the perfect cover for me. So I used it, yes, I did. I used it to my greatest advantage."

She looked at Dutch. "I never meant to hurt you. But I was young and there was so much pressure on me. From your mother and your father--"

"And from me," Dutch added for her.

"And from you, yes. I felt the pressure from you too. And everybody was billing this as if it was going to be the marriage on the century, from Nantucket to Cape Cod. It was just too much. I didn't know if I was ready for all of that responsibility. So I cracked under the weight and just couldn't face this place anymore."

"Did you plan to stay away this long?"

"No. Yes. I don't know, Dutch, I didn't have a plan. I just floated around for a few days, staying in this villa and that villa, especially after I found out the plane had crashed and there were no survivors. I made the decision then to let that fact, that there were no survivors, be my new reality. So I just floated from there. By the time I met Pierre I was a different woman, Dutch. I was independent and was just glad to float. I didn't want any responsibilities. But then I made the mistake of falling in love. We were married. And then the roof caved in."

"In the form of his fraudulent business dealings."

Caroline nodded. "Right. And just like I told you earlier, it just devastated me. I was left with nothing. I was literally poverty stricken. After divorcing him, I didn't know where to turn. My parents, I guess I should say my adopted parents, had since died, I had no siblings that I knew about, so I reached out to your mother. And here we are."

She covered her mouth as the tears returned, and she quickly stood to her feet. Dutch stood too, as he saw the emotion in her eyes.

"I never meant to hurt you, Dutch," she said through her tears. "I was just so lost then, just so . . ." She leaned against his chest. At first he just stood there, not knowing quite what to do, and then he wrapped her into his arms.

His heart hammered as he held her. This was *Caroline*, not any woman. This was the first woman he had loved so completely that he gave his heart to her. He not only loved and wanted to marry her, but had every intention of marrying her. He had asked her, she had said yes, they had planned their wedding down to the last detail. Her trip to France was her and his mother's idea, a chance for her to make last minute preparations on their honeymoon Villa.

For years a small part of Dutch blamed his mother for Caroline's death; for the fact that she was the one who encouraged her to go on that trip, a trip that ended in that fiery, horrific plane crash. He never dreamed she wasn't among the dead; that she had decided not to return to him. And he still could hardly believe that she was here, alive, and back in his loving arms.

Caroline knew by that look on Dutch's face that her tears had hit a nerve with him. He still loved her. She saw it in his eyes. But did he want her? That was what she needed to know. And that was why, as she leaned closer into him, she purposely rubbed her body against his groin, rubbed it in the expert way she had perfected from years of being his woman, and being married to a man just as virile as Dutch. Was he still that virile? Did he still respond to her the way he used to?

Within seconds, she got her answer. He began to engorge so quickly, she thought with an inward smile, that she wouldn't have been a bit surprised if that thick, juicy manhood of his would have popped out of his zipper.

But he realized it too, she decided, because he suddenly moved back from her, severing their sudden sensual contact. She looked at him. He handed her his handkerchief.

"What's the matter?" she asked, wiping her tears away.

"Nothing's the matter," he said in an almost defensive tone. "Are you all right?"

She nodded. "It's just so great seeing you again. I didn't think it could be possible."

He looked her dead in the eye, studying her, his green eyes so intense she wondered if he could see right through her, right straight through to her plotting and scheming. "I got married, too," he said to her.

That wasn't the words she had expected to come out of his mouth. "Did you?"

"While you were away, in France. I got married too."

"Yes, Dutch, I know. The world knows."

"Her name is Regina, as I'm sure you also know." Dutch wanted to make himself clear. He stared into her eyes. "She's the love of my life, Caroline, a wonderful, kind woman. There has never been anyone like her and never will." And, as if to put a nail in the coffin of any ideas she might have about them getting back together or being anything more than friends, he added: "I would like for you to meet her."

If Caroline had any doubts, his declaration of love for Gina was supposed to have removed them all. She, instead, removed herself from his arms. And stared right back at him. She wasn't accustomed to being rebuked by a man. She, in fact, in all of her life, had never been rebuked by any man. Her husband Pierre always craved her, Dutch used to always crave her, all of the men she hired to work around her home in France whenever her husband was away on business, craved her. And once she got every one of those men in her bed, and showed them what she could do, they craved her even more. She knew she was a sex addict. She knew she had to have it and have it repeatedly and by different men because one man was never enough to satisfy her own craving.

But she was getting older now. And afraid of being alone now. Sex for her was no longer a toy. After Pierre's betrayal, it was now the only weapon she had if she ever was going to experience that pure happiness she knew she would have had if his mother hadn't had a private eye following her, and taped her sex sessions with all of those other men.

But his mother was right. He would play hard to get initially, as the shock of seeing her alive and well began to take hold. But give it time, Victoria had told her. He'd come around. He'd compare her to that *person* he was married to, a woman who couldn't keep herself out of trouble to save her life, and who had caused him nothing but problems even before he said I Do. There was no doubt in Victoria's mind, she had insisted to Caroline, that he'd come around.

There was some doubt in Caroline's mind, however, especially now that he was obviously excited by her but was still able to restrain himself. There was a time when Dutch had so little restraint when it came to her body. And given how rapidly he had engorged when she rubbed against him, she had absolutely expected him to carry her upstairs and fuck her brains out, the way he used to do her; the way she was beginning to crave for him to do to her again.

But he didn't do it. He, instead, pulled back. Caroline, however, wasn't completely offended. She knew her value. She knew that it would be just a matter of time before he would be hers again. Especially if that so-called wife of his, according to Victoria and what she herself was able to find out from press reports, was as horrid as she seemed.

"Yes," she said to Dutch, smiling that smile he used to find so sexy; smiling grandly in an attempt to keep her true feelings completely her own. "I'd love to meet her. Truly I would."

TEN

Dutch sat at the head of his mother's lunch table and couldn't seem to take his eyes off of Caroline. He still couldn't completely wrap his brains around this. She was alive? It still seemed impossible to him. He remembered getting the news of the plane crash. He, his father, his mother and Max sat in the morning room waiting for answers. Were there any survivors, he would ask when he wanted to ask if Caroline survived, but was too terrified to be that specific. He remembered his father sitting beside him on the sofa, putting his arm around him, comforting him, seemingly as crushed by the news as he was.

And he remembered getting the word from French officials: no survivors. None. All, they said, were basically incinerated within the wreckage of the plane, somewhere on that mountain. Cooked like meat, he remembered his father mumbling. Cooked like meat.

"But it's true," Victoria, who sat at the opposite head of the table, said. "Walter, isn't it true?"

Max and Caroline, who sat at the table also, looked at Dutch. Dutch, who had been staring at Caroline more than he had been listening to any around-the-table conversation, looked at his mother. "Sorry?"

Victoria smiled at his inability to pay attention to anything but his woman. This was even easier than she thought it would be. "Caroline. Isn't she as beautiful as the day she stepped onto that plane?"

Dutch raked up a few peas and moved to put them in his mouth. "Yes," he said as he ate. He said it because it was true. She was as beautiful now as she was then. Older, yes, just as he was older, but she still had that extra something that always made her so alluring to him. But what was odd to him wasn't the fact that he still found her attractive: her attractiveness was just a fact in and of itself. But what surprised him the most was that his love for Caroline, which he thought had been so absolute and strong, seemed almost weak and feeble when compared to his love for Gina. Because there was no comparison. None.

But even with that, Caroline still managed to give him a rise. That concerned him. All she had to do was press that lithe little body of hers against him and his penis was ready to jut out of his pants and penetrate her. For a quick, unthinking moment he actually had wanted to fuck her. He had wanted to feel what it was like to be inside of her again. That was a first since his marriage to Gina, and that concerned him. Why would he even have considered such a thing? No woman compared to his woman. None. But he had truly wanted Caroline.

She was alluring, yes; he'd admit she was very alluring. But so were many women he knew and had to associate with sometimes on a daily basis. They never gave him any rise. Of course he had been in love with this particular woman, had made plans to marry and protect her for the rest of her life. And when he thought she had died, as when most loved ones die, the memory of her became embedded in his brain as some kind of perfection personified. Only her good was remembered. So he intellectually understood why he would react a little stronger sexually toward her than he did to any other woman outside of his wife.

But it still concerned him.

"When she first walked into this home," his mother continued, "I could hardly believe my eyes. 'Caroline?' I said aloud. 'Is that you, Caroline?' It took quite some time for me to get over it. Just as it will for you, too, Walter."

Caroline smiled. "Dutchie looked like he had seen a ghost," she said jovially. Dutch smiled too.

"It was rather shocking," he said.

"And Maxwell was even worst," Victoria said and they all laughed. When the laughter died down, she added: "But we are so very happy to have you back, Caroline. Your parents, God rest their souls, would have been so happy."

Caroline nodded. "I know. And I feel so terrible that I didn't even let them know anything. But I wasn't myself back then." She wasn't very close with nor cared much for her adopted parents to begin with, and that was the real reason she felt no obligation to them, and Victoria Harber knew it. But she was determined to keep the charade going.

"You were overwrought," Victoria said. "I was telling Walter, I was telling your parents, I was telling everybody that something was wrong with you, that they were stressing you to the max. But nobody listened to me."

"It was my fault," Caroline said. "I was taking on too much."

"Nonsense! You were a soon-to-be-bride so in love you could hardly think straight." *Could sleep with every Tom, Dick, and Harry*, Victoria inwardly thought as she said that, *but you certainly weren't thinking straight*. "It was a lot on someone so young."

She wasn't all that young, Max was thinking when his cell phone began to ring. He stood and moved away from the table to answer it. Ed Drake, National Security Advisor, only gave him a code. He closed his phone and immediately turned to the president.

He was laughing at some joke Caroline had told. "If you think the French people are arrogant, you should meet their president. That man never talks to me when we're together, he lectures me. Loves to call me son. He's got a few years on me, yes, but not that many."

"They treat me the same way some times," Caroline said as Dutch began to turn his attention to Max. "Americans, they seem to say," she continued, looking at Max too, "what do they know?"

"Yes?" Dutch asked his best friend who now had that serious, *I'm the chief of staff* look.

"It's nine o clock, sir," Max said and it was all he needed to say. The president immediately tossed his napkin on the table and stood to his feet.

"What's the matter, son?" Victoria asked him.

"I need to get back to Washington."

"Oh," Victoria said, thinking fast as Dutch walked over and kissed her on the cheek. Their relationship, ever since his marriage to Gina, had been quite contentious. But even he had to admit that his mother was at least attempting to make some amends.

He turned toward Caroline next, who stood to her feet. "I'm really happy, still shocked," he said with a smile, "but happy to see you alive and well." He reached over, to also kiss her gently on the cheek, but she moved her mouth just enough that his kiss landed on her lips. Victoria thought that such a move was very deft of her. Dutch, however, stepped back from her.

Victoria looked at Max. She had agreed to financially assist his political ambitions, but, as she also made clear, her money didn't come free. By that look on her face, Max had a sneaking suspicion that she was calling in one of those payments already.

"Sir," he said to the president. Dutch looked at him.

"I think she will need to come too. So we can decide how we're going to handle her return." Dutch looked puzzled. "Caroline's return, I mean.

The press could turn it into something we don't need to have to deal with."

Dutch nodded. "Okay. You're right, of course. Handle that, Max."

Fielding Reynolds, the president's personal assistant, also known as his "body" man, entered the dining hall. "It's nine o'clock, sir," he said.

Dutch began moving fast again. "Has everyone been contacted?" he asked Fielding.

"Yes, sir," Fielding said. "They're either on their way or in the Situation Room now. You're be briefed on Marine One."

Dutch, without looking back at his mother or his ex-fiancée, walked and talked with Fielding and left the hall.

"Surely we can't leave it like this," Victoria said, thinking fast, glancing at Caroline. Then she stood. "Max!" she called out to the chief of staff, who was leaving himself. "I wish to come too. To Washington I mean. To spend more time with my son."

When Max gave her a rather doubtful look, she added: "Caroline and I can share the Lincoln Bedroom if they don't have room."

Max smiled weakly. "Of course there's room. The president's mother is always welcome at the White House. There will always be room for you. But we'll have to leave now."

"Of course," Victoria said, moving from around the table, as she called for Nathan Riles.

Caroline quickly followed, but then touched Max rather sensually on his lower back to get him to stop walking while Victoria continued forward.

"What does 'nine o'clock' mean?" Caroline asked.

"Developments," Max said, and that was all he was going to say about it.

"I need your support, Maxwell," she said, her voice lowered.

"Support?"

"Yes."

"And what exactly am I supporting?"

"My bid to win my man back," she said without obfuscation. "What else?"

Max stared at her. "He's happily married, Caro. None of your wiles will work this time."

"Let me worry about that part. I just need you to stay out of my way. Put in an occasional encouraging word in his ear. Or," she added, straightening his always crooked tie, "that wondrous night we spent together all those years ago, while I was clearly still Dutch's woman, may just be revealed." She smiled after she said this, and walked away.

Max, knowing such a revelation would ruin him in every way possible, could barely stand.

By the time Max, Victoria and Caroline had arrived at the helipad on the outer edge of the Harber compound, Dutch was seated on Marine One and being briefed, on a secure phone link, by Ed Drake.

"Okay, Eddie, I'll see you shortly. And tell the team good job. Finally some good news." And then

144

Dutch hung up the phone, feeling hopeful for a change, as his body man removed the phone from his grasp.

He leaned back, looked at his mother and his resurrected former fiancée.

"Good news?" Caroline asked.

"Yes," he said. "I should rather think so."

Then she smiled that sexy smile he used to adore. And, to his horror, his penis began to throb.

The convoy of five SUVs left the Alan B. Polunsky prison with Gina, LaLa, and Christian in the fourth one. Gina was on the phone, with famed defense attorney Roman Wilkes, asking if he would get involved. When Roman agreed to look into the matter and then get back with her, she beamed. And hung up.

"Think that's a good idea?" LaLa asked her.

"You heard his story, La," Gina said. "I can't just hear him declare his innocence with information that could so easily be checked out, and do nothing."

"But even he admitted he used to sell drugs."

"Yes, he used to. But if his story is right, he turned his life around, had a legitimate job. Let's not forget, LaLa, that that's what Block by Block Raiders was all about: helping criminals make a new start. Marcus Rance would be a textbook example of what we were trying to do."

"If his story is true," LaLa pointed out.

"Right. If it all checks out. That's why I called Wilkie. He's the best defense attorney around. He'll get to the bottom of it without alerting the press and turning this into some kind of a media circus."

Christian snorted.

Gina looked at him. "What is it, Christian?"

"I mean," Christian said, smiling, "he's known as creating a circus around every case he tries."

"That ain't all he's known for," LaLa threw in.

Gina ignored her. "That's because the cases he tries are generally poor people already declared guilty in the court of public opinion. Mr. Wilkes has to change that perception, and the only way he can do it is to court the court of public opinion, so to speak. Trust me, he knows what he's doing."

"But do you?" LaLa asked.

Gina looked at her. "Our past relationship will have nothing to do with this. This isn't about us. This is about Marcus Rance."

"But that man couldn't keep his hands off of you when y'all used to date."

"If what Marcus said to us is true, he could have been falsely accused, La. I can't turn my back on that. And I can't hire just anybody. Because the attorney who takes on a case like this can't just be good. He's got to be great, like Roman Wilkes, because if there was any man that was guilty as sin in the court of public opinion, it's Marcus Rance. I have to make sure that he didn't go the way so many of our BBR clients went and was found guilty just because of his past sins."

Bam!!!

It sounded like a rocket hit and the SUV just in front of Gina's flew into the air, flipped over and over and dropped in a crash on the side of the road, and then began to roll like a mighty toy. The secret service agent riding in the front seat of Gina's SUV jumped to the back and threw her violently to the floor. The driver swerved to avoid the hit SUV, and just as he did the SUV behind them was hit too. It, too, flew into the air and flipped over and over. All Gina could hear, as she huddled on the floor, as LaLa and Christian huddled with her, was the sound of acceleration as her SUV seemed to go from fifty miles per hour to a hundred in a matter of nervous, heartrending seconds.

ELEVEN

Minutes before Gina's ordeal, Dutch and Max left the Situation Room and made their way to the White House residence. The hostages had been located and a strategy had been agreed upon. They would go in tomorrow night our time, under cover of darkness, with the best Seals team the military had to offer, and get them out. His SecDef and SecState gave him full assurances. Dutch felt rejuvenated. But he felt extremely antsy too.

"You look full of yourself," his mother said as he entered the second floor residence. She and Caroline were seated on the sofa.

Dutch laughed as he headed for the bar. "Thank-you, Mother, for your kind words. Would either of you care for anything to drink?"

"We've been offered drinks," Caroline said, "but declined."

"What about you, Max?"

"No, I'm good," Max said as he sat in the chair flanking the sofa. "How do you like the digs, Caroline?" he asked. "I understand they took you on a tour."

"They did. And I love it. Quite gorgeous actually. And not nearly as formal as I would have thought."

Dutch poured himself a glass of wine and then took a seat in the chair across from the sofa.

"What was the big meeting about?" Caroline wanted to know.

Dutch crossed his legs. "Work and more work," he said.

"Did you ever pursue your photography while you lived in France, Caro?" Max asked.

Caroline smiled. They are so secretive around here, she thought. "A little, early on, and then no. I was too busy being a wife."

Knocks were heard on the sitting room door. Max answered it. And then stepped outside of the room, closing it behind him.

"Did you ever have children?" Victoria asked her. She and Dutch exchanged glances.

"No, I did not. We, my husband actually, couldn't have any."

"That's too bad."

"Did you want any?" Dutch asked and stared at her to see if she had changed. There was a time when she had jokingly promised to give him ten babies. "But at least two," he remembered she loved to say.

"Yes," she said. "Lots. But at least two."

Dutch sipped from his wine.

"There's still time," Victoria said, patting her hand. "You're still a young woman."

Max reentered the sitting room, looking flustered to everyone, as he made his way up to the president's chair. "May I see you for a moment, sir?" he asked.

Dutch at first seemed annoyed by Max's interruption. Until he saw that flustered look on his face.

"Yes, of course," he said, excused himself, and he and Max went into the small, private office within the residence, an office specifically designed for the president's personal use.

"What is it?" he asked his chief of staff as soon as the door closed.

"A call just came in, sir," Max said and seemed to wait for Dutch to ask a question. Dutch, however, remained silent. It couldn't be the rescue mission they had just worked out since such a mission wouldn't commence until five thirty pm tomorrow night our time, 3am Afghanistan's.

"It's your wife, sir," Max continued, and although Dutch remained calm outwardly, Max knew him long enough to see that sudden stormy look that came into his eyes.

"What about my wife?" Dutch asked, barely able to contain himself.

"She was being escorted from the Polunsky prison when her convoy of SUVs came under attack--"

Dutch stepped back a step, his heart ramming against his chest.

"There was an attack," Max went on. "Two of the SUVs were hit. It was awful, according to the initial reports we're just getting in. All of the passengers in the two vehicles that were hit were killed."

"What about Gina? Is Gina all right?"

"Yes, she's all right. She wasn't hit. They had wanted her to go to Walter Reed as a precaution, but she refused. Mainly because physically she's fine. She's flying back to Andrews now."

"With Fighter Jet escort?"

"You'd better believe it, sir. Ed just assured me."

Dutch rubbed his forehead, his eyes beginning to flutter. This was unbelievable. Gina had been at risk? Gina? His *wife*?

"Christian and LaLa were with her," Max said, causing Dutch to look up at him. Only that calm, reassuring look he was known for was gone. He looked more perplexed than self-assured.

"They okay?" Dutch asked.

"They're okay too," Max said.

"Prepare Marine One," Dutch ordered. "I'm going to meet her plane."

"Until they can determine the source of the attack, sir, the Secret Service asks that you remain in the White House."

"Prepare Marine One," Dutch said again. "I'm going to meet her plane."

Max knew it was a futile fight anyway. "Yes, sir," he said, and left.

Dutch stood there, unable to get a grip on anything, especially his fast-surfacing anxiety and guilt. And when he moved to walk, he stumbled into a shelf of books.

He stayed where he stumbled, leaned against those books, his hands now covering his face in anguish. And all he could think about was Gina, and the awfulness of her ordeal, and the fact that, but for her being married to him, she would have never been in any such danger.

"Dear Lord," he said aloud. "What have I done?"

Although he spoke to her by phone during his entire helicopter ride over to Andrews Air Force Base, and she had reassured him that she was completely untouched, he still felt an anguish that ripped at his soul. When he walked toward the plane, with Max and Dempsey just behind him, and saw her appear and begin to dismount, he ran.

He ran across the field, ran up the steps of the plane taking two at a time, ran like the athlete he used to be. Gina ran too, and at mid-step, when they met, they embraced.

His heart pounded as he held her, as his eyes closed tightly in thankful prayer to God for returning her safely to him. Then he looked at her. Looked anxiously at her.

"Are you truly all right?" he asked her with all earnestness, his green eyes unable to stop scanning every inch of her.

"I'm truly all right," she said. And she was, except for the terror that sparkled like an unshed tear in her bright brown eyes.

When Marine One landed on the helipad within the South Lawn of the White House, Victoria and Caroline, who had to find out about this incredible ordeal from cable news accounts, who didn't even know that Dutch had left the White House to go and meet his wife's plane, stood at the entrance on the South Portico.

"I told you she was a camera hog," Victoria was telling an upset Caroline. "Your return back into the president's life, which would have been the big news, and what does she do? Manage to get herself attacked, that's what. It's all so very distasteful."

"That's her, isn't it?" Caroline asked as Dutch and Gina stepped out of the helicopter, flanked by military officials, and began walking across the South Lawn. Dutch had his arm tightly wrapped around his wife's waist, and Gina had her head on her husband's shoulder. Physically she was unscathed. But emotionally she was beaten.

"That's her," Victoria said after looking and seeing the twosome herself. "That's who you are competing against, if you can believe it."

And Victoria, for once, Caroline thought, was right. *This* was her competition? Some tall, dark-skinned chick with far too many curves? What in the world could Dutch have seen in *her*? Caroline had studied her pictures, every one she could find on the internet, and had researched every interview she had given on television. But she still couldn't see the allure. But maybe, she had also thought, the woman would be better looking in person.

But looking at her now, as they made their way toward the porch of the South Portico, Caroline knew she had thought wrong. This woman had just been through a lot, no doubt about that, but that couldn't change the fact that she wasn't especially beautiful. That she was, from Caroline's vantage point, downright plain.

She smooth down her long, black hair, straightened her skintight dress, and waited for the introduction. She'd treat the lady with respect. She'd smile and put on a good show. But all the while she was going to be sizing up the competition, finding the weak spots, and then pouncing.

But that grand introduction she had been expecting never happened. Dutch, with his wife tightly against his side, entered the opened doors where Caroline and his mother stood, and didn't so much as acknowledge their presence with a nod of the head. He still had Gina wrapped in his arms, her head still remained on his shoulder with her eyes tightly shut, and they walked right past them.

Victoria immediately took umbrage as she could not believe the level of disrespect. Neither could Caroline, especially when you consider the woman in his arms.

"Can you believe that?" Caroline said, her attempt at civility gone. "He walked right by us as if we weren't even here! And that wife of his smelled of sweat. Sweat! And he pampers *her*?"

Victoria, however, ushered Caroline away from the doors and the listening ears of the guards. She was so embarrassed by that hideous son of hers that she could hardly bear it.

But Caroline was more than embarrassed. She was fuming. Who in the hell did he think he was playing with? That wife of his wasn't hurt in that attack, she was no longer in any danger. So why couldn't he stop for two seconds and say something? Even an *I'll talk to you later*, or even a nod of the head, would have been preferable to *nothing*.

But nothing was exactly what they received. Because, in truth, Dutch wasn't thinking about either one of them. Gina was all he was concerned about right here and right now. Even that hostage rescue couldn't get his attention right now. Because Gina was back. And his singular focus was to get her to their bedroom so that he could attempt to make her as comfortable, and as safe, as he possibly could.

She was with him now. That was all that mattered to him.

TWELVE

Not a word was spoken when they entered the master bathroom. Dutch had already ordered that a bath be drawn and ready for the First Lady, and it was. And as they stood in the middle of that bathroom and he undressed her, Gina seemed unable to take her hands off of him. If she had to move a hand so that he could unzip this, or untie that, she would put her other hand somewhere on his person. It was as if she felt almost helpless, and she hated it. But the memories were still there. The sight of that massive SUV lifting into the air before her very eyes, like a toy car in a movie, kept replaying itself in her head. She even thought she saw one of the agents fly through the windshield when the SUV slammed back down and began to roll, but no, they said, it was a trick of the eye. They all had on seatbelts. No one flew out.

But no-one survived, either.

She dismissed the thought as her husband lifted her into the warm water and her body relaxed to the feel. As she began to bathe herself, he seemed to be well aware of her nervousness. That was why he didn't leave her, but sat on the vanity chair inside of the bathroom and made his phone calls right where he sat.

His most contentious tongue-lashing came during a conference call with the DNI, his Director of

National Intelligence, and his Secretary of Homeland Security. Dutch wanted to know how in the world could rocket-propelled grenades get anywhere near the First Lady's convoy. Somebody had dropped the ball, Dutch made clear, and he wanted names. Both department heads, sufficiently humbled, swore to get to the bottom of it, promising that heads would roll. Dutch hung up. Once the dust cleared heads would roll all right, and it would begin with theirs.

As he sat there, his own head in his hands, his body so drained he could barely sit in that chair, he heard a muffled sound. When he looked up and realized Gina was just sitting there, in the tub, covered in suds and crying, his heart dropped.

"Oh, *darling*," he said and hurried to her, ready to step into that tub fully clothe if he had to, but realized he didn't and removed them.

He sat in behind her, wrapping her into his arms, and she leaned back against his hard frame and let it all out. She sobbed. She couldn't stop crying. People died today, men and women who were just doing their jobs, and there was no easy way to get over that. She leaned against her husband and held nothing back.

Dutch took her weight and allowed her the catharsis she needed. But it would be some time later, after he had finished bathing her himself, dried her off, put her in their bed, and after he had dried off too and got in bed with her, snuggling her closely to his chest, did his own emotions begin to release.

And when the tears came, they came as inwardly wrenching and outwardly silent as Dutch had always allowed his emotions to display. But as Gina lay against him, unaware of his catharsis, now so peaceful herself, he couldn't hold back. So many contradictory feelings warred against each other in his mind, including that ever-lurking possibility of resigning. That thought never left. Take his wife and get the hell out of this fishbowl forever.

But what terrified him was the truth of their dilemma. Because resigning wouldn't change a damn thing. Because even after he would no longer be president, even after they were as far away from Washington politics as they could get, he would still forever be the former President of the United States, and she would forever be its former First Lady. There would still be a target on her back. Time may blur its clarity and value, but it would still be there. Like a bell that had already rung. Like a symphony that had already played that song. They could never undo the fact that she had once been the First Lady of the United States of America. Never. And it was all because of his decision to marry her right away, while he was still president, while he was in a tough reelection fight that he refused to quit.

Now the love of his life had an eternal target on her back. And it was all because of him, he thought bitterly, as he stared at her beautiful ebony face. As he kissed her on the nose, snuggled her naked body closer against his naked frame, and laid his head on top of hers.

The next morning, to Dutch's surprise, his penis had found its way deep inside of Gina. It was, in fact, that feeling of sensual tightness that had awakened both of them from what had been an incredibly relaxing sleep. And as Gina began to rub her naked ass against his stomach, as she moved to the feel of his penis inside of her, Dutch began to gyrate too. They did nothing else but lay there and moved in a slow, relaxing, simple rhythm. They didn't talk; they didn't try to make it anything but what it was. A joining. A two-as-one coming together. The rocking of the bed they could hear. The sound of saturation they could hear. And it those sounds more than the lovemaking itself that did it, the sounds of his wetness mating with hers as they continually released, as they continually gyrated, as they continually moved physically and metaphysically closer and closer until both their bodies strained into a spiral of orgasm. Gina closed her eyes and cried. Dutch closed his eyes and cried too. Because it felt, not like a climax, but an affirmation.

They affirmed to live the rest of their lives as a twosome, no matter what missiles the world tossed at them. They affirmed to never again let there be any daylight between them no matter how many reasons there was to go their separate ways. And, most importantly of all, if it was the two of them against the world, then the world be damned. It was going to be the two of them.

It was an affirmation fraught with the pain of trauma, of Dutch almost losing the most important person in his life, and they understood that. But they affirmed it anyway.

And after that climax, after their affirmation, they lay on their backs in silence. It would be another long, drawn out period of time, minutes that felt like hours, before they would speak.

Gina turned to face him, her eyes narrowing in that sincere but disconcerting look of hers that always got his attention. And when she said, "good morning," and smiled that beautiful, bright white smile of hers, he relaxed too.

"Good morning."

"You realize it's after eight o clock?"

"I realize that."

"I'm surprised one of your aides hasn't come for you. You aren't usually anywhere near a bed by eight am."

You aren't usually under attack the day before, he wanted to say, but it was still too raw for him to make light of it. "How about that?" he said, instead.

"What's on tap today?" she asked, and he realized right away that she was trying to reclaim some normalcy. "Meetings and more meetings?"

"You know it. But we do have good news on the hostage front."

This piqued her interest. "What's happened?"

"Eyes only," he said, which she knew meant that the information he was giving her required clearance of the highest order. What the world didn't realize was that it was Gina, not his cabinet, not Max or Allison, who was his closest advisor. He told her everything that happened in his administration. Above all the king's men, he trusted her. "We know where the hostages are being held."

This was surprising indeed. "That's great news, Dutch," she said. "That's wonderful news."

"And," he added, "we're finalizing plans to secure their release."

Gina's heart pounded. "An inside source I take it?"

"You take it correctly."

"That's great, Dutch. Is an Al-Qaeda affiliate?"

"An even looser affiliate than we had initially thought, but yes."

Gina wanted to ask if that same organization was responsible for the attack on her convoy, but she couldn't bring herself to ask it. Dutch, however, who was staring at her, whose hand was rubbing her braids, answered her unasked question anyway.

"No," he said, "it wasn't the same group that attacked your convoy, darling. They wanted us to believe it was, to maximize their publicity no doubt, but no. My Intel people believe it was a copycat pure and simple, a homegrown terror group masquerading as an Al-Qaeda affiliate. They believe they know whom, also, but we'll see."

Gina closed her eyes, rested her forehead against his.

Max and the rest of his staff were already insisting, even as he journeyed over to Andrews to meet Gina's plane, that he parade her before the cameras, to reassure America that the First Lady was okay, but Dutch had nixed the idea in its infancy. Nobody was parading his wife anywhere, he had told them, and least of which in front of that man-eating press. He would brief the press himself and make clear that she was just fine. If that wasn't enough for them, then tough, he decided. He didn't give a shit.

"Was it as magnificently terrible as I believe it was?" Dutch carefully asked Gina after a few minutes of deafening silence, his fingers now tracing along her bare back and backside. He knew this was still a horrific memory for her, and always would be, but the only way he could help her, he believed, was to know exactly what she had gone through to begin with.

She nodded her head. "It was bad," she admitted. "I don't think terrible is a strong enough word for how bad it was. It was unbelievable. And when I found out that those men had died, that those good men. . ." She shook her head. "I can't, Dutch," she said, and looked into his eyes, tears forming in hers. He understood. And pulled her into his arms.

After another long period of silence, he slightly changed the subject.

"How did it go with Mr. Rance?" he asked her.

She smiled, which he took to be a good sign. "It was nothing like I expected it to be," she said. "He says he's innocent."

Dutch smiled. "Like every convicted killer."

"I know. But still."

Dutch looked down at her. "But still what?"

Gina hesitated. Had to remind herself that this wasn't about her, but about justice. "But I think it should be looked into, that's all."

Dutch stared at her. She was an advocate to her heart. And he wasn't about to trounce on that. He, in fact, loved that about her. "I don't want you looking into it," he did, however, make clear.

"No, not me. An old friend of mine." Gina hesitated before saying his name. "Roman Wilkes," she ultimately said.

Dutch knew Wilkes to be a famous criminal defense attorney, a smooth, good looking man of the bar. He also remembered the press attempting to romantically link Wilkes to Gina during the campaign. Gina admitted they used to be romantically linked, but years ago. And Dutch didn't comment on it now. He, instead, filed it away in the Rolodex of his mind to be retrieved, if needed, some other time.

"What exactly will Wilkes be looking into?" he asked Gina.

"Marcus is claiming that he was working at the time of that drive-by shooting, and that he has plenty of corroboration, including a co-worker and his boss. And as for DNA, according to him, I haven't confirmed any of this, but he says there was no DNA presented at trial. Just the fact that the assailant was driving his stolen vehicle."

Dutch frowned. "That's ridiculous, Regina. Why would the police arrest him if he could prove that he was at work at the time, especially if they had no scientific evidence?"

"It happens, Dutch. Believe me," she said, her passion released. "Witnesses come forward, but the jury just doesn't believe them because they aren't necessarily upstanding citizens themselves. In Marcus's case, all of the people who worked at that furniture delivery company had rough backgrounds, including, apparently, the owner. That's why the owner hired them. He had turned his life around, and was trying to help turn theirs around."

"But the idea that people would say that he didn't do it and there was no DNA that categorically said that he did, yet they still sentenced him to death? That's hard to believe, Gina."

"I know it is. That's why it happens more times than people think, because it just can't be true. But sometimes it is true. When I was running BBR, and looked into those cases, I was astounded too. I saw it more times than you would believe, Dutch. It happens."

Dutch still seemed doubtful.

"Remember the Geter case?"

"Not really, no," Dutch said.

"Well, this black engineer, Lenell Geter, was accused of armed robbery, in Texas too, and sentenced to life in prison. Forget that he was at work at the time. Forget that he had co-workers willing to testify on his behalf, they sentenced him anyway. If it wasn't for that Morley Safer report on 60 Minutes back in the eighties, which exposed this kind of craziness, that man would have probably still been in jail to this day for something he didn't do.

And don't forget all of these inmates that the Innocence Project has freed; men who've served fifteen, twenty years for murders they didn't commit. It happens, Dutch."

Dutch studied her. This was her passion. This was what she did. The fact that it was her half-brother probably heightened her interest and was probably the reason why she asked Wilkes to help, despite the rumors. He was undoubtedly the best at this sort of case and Dutch knew her to be the kind of woman who would put herself out there, in the grind of the rumor mill again, to help somebody else. Especially, as she put it, her father's son.

"Just don't get too caught up in this, Regina," he ordered her. "I don't want you out there railing against something that may not be what Rance is making it out to be. Wait for the facts, and consult me before you go public with any of it. Understand?" he said this and looked at her.

She smiled. "Understood," she said. Then she continued to look at him, the terror of last night still planted in her brain. Also planted was the fact that Dempsey had phoned LaLa just after they left the prison and mentioned that Dutch's mother and some very beautiful woman had come back from Nantucket with him. Gina didn't call Dutch to find out what that was about, but had opted to wait until she got back home to see for herself.

Now the suspense was killing her.

"How did it go for you? At Nantucket, I mean?"

Dutch's heart hammered against his chest for some reason. "It went okay," he said. "My mother decided to come back to Washington with me."

"Yeah, I heard."

Dutch looked at her. "Do you have a problem with that?"

Gina considered his question. "A problem? No. I don't like her, and she can't stand me, but she's your mother. Your mother will always be welcomed wherever we live."

Dutch loved her so much. "Thank-you," he said. Then he wrinkled his brow. "She didn't come alone," he said. "There's been a new development."

It was Gina's heart that hammered this time. Was this that other shoe? Was this beautiful, mystery woman some old girlfriend of the president's? Was he going to tell her that he was in love with this woman and wanted a divorce? It was highly unlikely to Gina, the way he held her last night, and their affirmation this morning seemed to seal the unlikeliness, but given the way her life often went she wasn't about to put anything past anyone.

She stared at him.

"Her name is Caroline Parker."

Gina was puzzled. "Caroline Parker? But isn't that the woman. . ." It made no sense. But she remembered that name. Had even Googled that name and stared at the beautiful photos of her on the Internet, all proclaiming her to be the president's great lost love. She swallowed hard. "Isn't that the name of the woman, of your fiancée who had died in that plane crash?"

Dutch nodded, a painful look crossing his handsome face. "Yes," he said.

"But. . . What are you telling me, Dutch? Are you telling me that she didn't die? That she's alive?"

"That's what I'm telling you, yes."

"So she wasn't on the plane at all?"

"She was on the plane when it landed in France. But she didn't come back. She stayed in France. The flight manifest wasn't changed, and so when the plane crashed, there was no survivor to tell us that she stayed back."

Gina still couldn't understand this. "But she survived. If she stayed back, she survived. Why didn't she tell y'all?"

Dutch exhaled. He felt the same way. "She said the reason she stayed back was because she couldn't face it anymore."

"Face what?"

"The pressure of the wedding. In our circles it didn't get any bigger than our wedding. And she said it was becoming too much for her. Her plan, if she had one, was to stay away for a while, travel around France under assumed names so that I wouldn't know where she was or come looking for her. At least not until she could gather the strength to face me. But then the plane crashed, she was presumed dead too, so she decided, with no aforethought, she claims, to keep it that way."

"To stay dead?"

"Yes."

"So what brought her back alive?" Gina wanted to know.

Dutch would have smiled if he hadn't asked the exact same question. "Her French husband was convicted of some major securities fraud; they lost everything, including the very roof over her head. And so she reached out to my mother."

"Who, I'm sure, given how she feels about me, welcomed her back with loving arms."

Dutch didn't respond to that, and Gina immediately regretted the fact that she just exposed her anger. Instead of celebrating the fact that the woman was alive, she was actually upset by this revelation.

"Why did your mother," Gina said, careful to keep her irritation in check, "decide to bring this Caroline Parker to Washington with her?"

"To break up our marriage so that Caroline and I could be together again."

Gina looked at Dutch, amazed by his clarity. He even smiled, which caused her to smile, albeit nervously.

"And those two schemers," he said with a laugh, "thought I was just that clueless. They actually believe they're getting one over on me."

Gina laughed this time. "So why did you let them come here, if you knew what they were up to?"

"Because I want you and me in a room with Caroline and my mother so that I can make it clear, with no misunderstandings, no second hand information, that they had better get any notions of undermining my marriage out of their pretty little heads. We have enough demons to battle. We aren't battling them, too."

Gina's eyes narrowed as she stared at her husband. And here she was, thinking she was unlucky when, because of Dutch's love, she might just be the luckiest woman of them all.

But tears were in her eyes after he pulled her into his arms. Because she just couldn't see it. Because she just knew that even a *come-to-Jesus* meeting with those two wouldn't end it. Not if that mother of his was involved. Gina knew that witch, and unlike Jennifer Caswell who went away quietly, she was more than a force of nature. She was evil. And the forces of evil could be the most potent foe.

They were not out of the woods yet.

THIRTEEN

When Gina arrived at the breakfast table later that morning, she wasn't at all surprised to see the two women staring daggers at her. But what she was surprised to find was that Caroline Parker, even more than a decade after those photos she had seen of her were taken, was still a remarkably beautiful sight to behold. Her heart that had soared when Dutch confessed his knowledge of their scheme and how it wasn't going to work, came back down to earth a bit when she saw Caroline.

Caroline's heart had the opposite effect. Last night, after Dutch arrived at the White House with the First Lady and didn't so much as acknowledge her when they walked by, she began to wonder if she stood any chance with that man. But this morning, seeing Regina Lansing, not just after some ordeal, but freshly scrubbed and dressed in another one of those ridiculous African outfits she favored, her heart actually soared. Because she believed that the odds of her taking Dutch away from this woman were excellent. She believed she more than stood a chance.

"Good morning," Victoria said when Gina finally joined them for breakfast. Not that she could eat a thing. She couldn't. But she, like them, wanted to get a firsthand look at her enemies.

"Good morning," she said as the chef brought her the cup of coffee and toast she had ordered before she even arrived in the room.

"That's all you're eating?" Victoria asked as she patted her mouth with her napkin. She and Caroline both were very petite women, and both appeared to have moved around more than ate the little food they did have on their plates. "It seems painfully obvious that you generally eat more."

Caroline smiled. Gina chomped on her toast. "So you're Caroline?" she said.

"Yes," Caroline said, surprised that she would put it that way. "And you're Regina Lansing."

Gina simply looked at her. So she wanted to play it that way, did she? She could have corrected the wench. Could have told her that no, I'm actually Regina *Harber*, the *First* Lady. But she didn't have the desire to even go there.

"Where's the president?" Victoria asked.

"In a meeting," Gina said, still remembering how welcoming it felt to have his arms around her all night; how wonderful it was to awake to the feel of his penis inside of her this morning.

"In a meeting already?" Victoria asked. "My goodness. Where has his manners gone? The least he could have done was to say hello to his household guests this morning. Especially after last night."

They both glanced at Gina, as if begging her to ask about last night. That was why she chomped again on her toast, and didn't.

Caroline, in fact, was amazed at how she wasn't asking her any questions. Your husband's long-lost fiancée suddenly appears and you aren't interested? Unless, Caroline thought a little less aggressively, Dutch had told her all she felt she needed to know.

Victoria, however, knew there was a button to push somewhere on this female, and she was determined to find it. "Did he say when he would get back with us?" she wanted to know.

Gina thought about this. "No," she said, remembering nothing to that effect.

"Not a word? I find that rather hard to believe."

"Then don't believe it. But it's a fact."

Victoria didn't like her tone. In any other context a woman like her would be serving her, not sitting at a table with her, and would know the difference. "I understand you endured a harrowing experience yesterday," she decided to try. "If the press reports are accurate."

Gina stared at her, wondering where was she going with what she knew was ultimately a line of attack.

"According to those reports," Victoria continued when Gina just looked at her, "you were visiting your brother, the murderer."

Bingo, Gina thought and actually smiled. "Yes, I was," she said.

"They commuted his sentence to life in prison, Caroline," Victoria continued, "thanks to her friendship with the Governor of Texas."

"Really? I'm certain that didn't help Dutch politically, a move like that. When I was his woman, before he was even considering politics, I would have known better than to do anything that would shed an unfavorable light on him. Especially having the sentence of a murdered commuted. And then to visit him? That's just not done in our circles."

"Precisely," Victoria said, and looked at Gina. "As I'm sure you are now aware, Caroline was the love of Dutch's life before the plane crash. They were deeply in love and were to be married. Then tragedy struck. But, fortunately for me and Dutch, who love Caroline, she's back with us. What it means for your future is an open question, of course. Dutch and Caroline will have to come together and make a decision on that in the next few days. But I just want you to know right here and right now that I will fight you with every breath in my body if you attempt, in any way, to obstruct the great love my son and Caroline have for each other. I'll not allow your hijinks to overshadow their great love because believe you me the American people will be squarely behind their union as vociferously as they oppose any relationship you might think you have with my son."

Gina just sat there. This woman sounded as if she was living in a parallel universe where Caroline could just pick up where she left off and Gina's marriage to Dutch never happened. It was so outside of anything common sensible that Gina didn't even bother to respond to it. She drank the last of her coffee, wiped her hands on the napkin, and stood to leave. It was a stunned Caroline, however, who interrupted her decampment.

"Wait a minute," she said and Gina turned toward her. "I'm a little confused. You do understand that I was Dutch's fiancée? The one he thought was dead?"

"Yes, I understand that."

"Well, do you have any questions for me?"

Gina stared at her. These people, Caroline and Victoria, were so accustomed to the world kowtowing to their every need, that they were utterly stumped when someone didn't. And Gina wasn't about to. If this wasn't the White House, if Dutch wouldn't end up taking a serious political hit for her actions, if Victoria wasn't Dutch's own mother, she would have kicked both their asses to the curb.

"No," she said. "Do you have any questions for me?"

Caroline looked at Gina as if she had just grown a third head. "Why would I have questions for you?" she asked Gina.

"Why would I have questions for you?" Gina asked her. Then smiled when Caroline was again taken aback, and left.

Later that day, in her office in the East Wing, she relayed everything that had happened to LaLa and Christian. Neither one of them could believe it.

"Did you have questions for *her*?" LaLa asked. "Where does that chick get off?"

"Oh, she's a beautiful woman. She's got it going on all right," Gina said, her arms folded, sitting behind her desk. "You should see her. Those pictures of her on the Internet do her no justice."

"I heard she was a looker," Christian said, "and that the president loved her so completely."

LaLa elbowed Christian, but she needn't have bothered. Gina didn't exactly want to hear any more talk of the president's great love for that woman, but it was a fact. He did, back in the day, loved her. For Dutch to have asked the woman to marry him meant that she had something he liked well enough to make her his queen. But that crown, Gina also knew, now belonged to her.

"What do you think she wants?" LaLa asked, standing, with Christian, in front of the desk.

"Dutch, what else?" Gina said forthrightly. "She wants Dutch back."

"But she can't have him," Christian blurted out and both Gina and LaLa smiled.

"No, Christian," Gina said, "she can't. And won't."

"So why are you and the president allowing her to stay here?"

"Because, young man, when you're president and First Lady, everything has to be managed. He couldn't allow her to stand on that vast estate in Nantucket and confess her continued love for President Harber, with his mother standing beside her in full agreement that my marriage should be annulled or something equally ridiculous so that Caroline can take her rightful place beside her rightful man."

"That's crazy," Christian said with a smile.

"Yes, it is," LaLa said, "but honey, if you haven't learned anything since coming to Washington you'd better learn this: these people of privilege like this Caroline person and the president's mother are just that crazy. They live in a bubble and expect you to conform to that bubble. Yes, sir, it's nuts, but so are they. They see people like us as nothing more than pawns in their game. They get to make all of the moves. We just have to get out of the way."

"What about the president?" Christian asked. "Where's he? Does he understand what's going on?"

"He understands perfectly," Gina said with a smile.

"Did you see his press conference this morning?" LaLa asked Gina.

"No, why?"

"It was all about you, that's why. All about the ambush, of course, but also about why he allowed you to go and see a murderer. Or, as they put it, *the* murderer, as if no other human in the annals of history has ever committed such a crime." Then LaLa looked at Gina. "Speaking of which," she said, "Roman Wilkes called."

Gina looked at LaLa. "Oh, yeah? And what did he want?"

"A meeting. Says he uncovered some very interesting information."

"Oh, my," Gina said, knowing that any truth to Marcus's claim would be great for Marcus, but terrible for her and Dutch and their life in this fishbowl, "then it's true?"

"He didn't go that far. But he sounds as if he's on to something."

"Set it up."

"For when? Tonight?"

Gina remembered Dutch saying that they were putting the final touches on that hostage rescue. "No, not tonight. Tomorrow maybe, or the day after. I want Dutch present when we meet."

"Will do," LaLa said. "You want me there, too?"

Gina smiled. "Why? You have to get permission from Demps to come?"

"Hell nall. Why would you say that?"

"Even before that ambush yesterday, he seemed rather protective of you."

"Yeah, they always do when something's undercover. To make sure you ain't doing it too."

"Excuse me?" Gina said, puzzled.

"Nothing girl. But anyway, I'll set it up." And LaLa, as if to avoid any further scrutiny, was gone.

"What was that all about?" Christian asked.

But Gina didn't answer. Because she really didn't know.

FOURTEEN

The president stood behind the podium in the East Room of the White House, the press assembled to ask questions afterwards, and read from the teleprompter. It was ten pm and his remarks were being carried live on every channel in the country. The networks had been alerted that the news was big, and worthy of the coverage, but it was only after receiving confirmation from the Vice President himself did they agree to interrupt their prime time shows to cover what they now knew would not be a routine press conference.

The president began, looking nervous his mother thought, as she, Caroline, Christian and Gina looked at the press conference from the television in the residence. He looked gorgeous, Caroline thought, as she was becoming more anxious to have him now. The money Victoria had promised her was awesome and needful, but Dutch could give her so much more. More money, more hot sex, more everything. And it appeared to be working. Other than last night, their few interactions since her return had been very positive. But they hadn't interacted at all since his wife hit the scene, a wife Caroline found almost insufferable. Dutch married *that*, she at one point wanted to blurt out. It was almost embarrassing to her that a woman of that low quality, a woman who was a total non-factor as far as she was concerned, would be her competition.

Dutch, however, singularly focused on the task at hand, began his prepared remarks. "At exactly five thirty pm eastern standard time, three am Afghanistan time, a team of U.S. Navy SEALS stormed a compound in the Helmand Province of Afghanistan and rescued the captured American hostages. A gun battle did ensue, but our SEALS team was able to overcome them all. All six students and three businessmen that remained are now in US custody and their captors have been killed. We would like to thank the Afghan government and, of course, our men and women in uniform, for their brave and courageous actions."

As Dutch began taking questions, Gina's cell phone rang. She moved over by the bar, to get away from the loud television, only to hear a very distraught LaLa on the other end.

"What's the matter, girl?" she asked her best friend.

"I have proof," LaLa said.

"Excuse me?"

"I have proof," LaLa said again. "How could he do this to me, Gina? After all these years how could he do this to me?"

Gina knew it was about Dempsey, and based on the pain in LaLa's voice, she knew it was bad.

"Can you come over?" LaLa ultimately asked her.

Gina "coming over" was no longer as simple as getting in a car and going, and LaLa, as Gina's personal assistant, knew it better than anyone else. She wouldn't have asked if it wasn't vital.

"Yes, of course," Gina replied. "I'm on my way."

She closed her cell phone, watched her husband answer press questions about the details of the raid itself, and then pulled Christian aside. Although their conversation was meant to be private, Victoria and Caroline listened with rapt attention to every word. Gina ordered him to contact the Secret Service and make the necessary arrangements. Given how LaLa sounded, given that Demps was still out of town, Gina also told him that she was probably going to stay the night with her friend.

When she and Christian gave their apologies for their abrupt departure and left the sitting room, Victoria looked at the younger woman. Dutch's voice, and the voice of reporters asking questions, droning on in the background.

"You know what this means?" Victoria said.

Caroline looked at her. "This is my chance?"

"This is the night. He'll be on such a high because of this hostage release story, which means he will more than likely be the perfect happy fool."

Caroline smiled. "What do you mean?"

"Get him, that's what I mean," Victoria said in no uncertain terms. "He will be unawares. He won't see it coming until he's practically inside of you making, if the stars line up, a beautiful, healthy, *white* baby boy. And if the child isn't conceived on your first mating, he'll surely want more of you thereafter. You know my son. I remember how he couldn't keep his hands off of you."

"Perhaps he's changed," Caroline said, not believing it herself.

"Nonsense!" Victoria said. "People don't change. You were his first great love, his only true love as far as I'm concerned. And that's why this has got to work. You have got to earn your money tonight. Tonight will be the beginning of the end of that sham of a marriage. Because I will tell you and anybody else that I'll not sit idly by and let that black wench get what she wants. There will be no little black boy who grows up to marry a little black girl and those blacks end up with everything me and my husband has ever worked for. And it'll be theirs? Over my dead body! You will mate with Walter Harber, you hear me? And ultimately the two of you, the only one I know he has ever loved and still loves, will produce that magnificent baby."

A magnificent *white* baby, Caroline thought. She wants herself a white grandchild. Is willing to give up big bucks to make it happen. Is willing to ruin her son's sham of a marriage, as she calls it, to ensure that no dark-skinned woman chocolate-up that vanilla bloodline. And ironically enough she wanted Caroline, whom Victoria, like most of the families in their Nantucket circle, knew was half-black herself, to keep that "pure" white line.

But that was Victoria Harber, Caroline thought with a sneer: a living, breathing, eerily absurd contradiction.

Gina and LaLa sat in the quiet living room of LaLa's Georgetown home, one woman on one sofa, the other woman on the opposite sofa. Christian was there too, seated at the dining room table in the home with the open floor plan, and the Secret Service, as usual, had the home blanketed with security, although no one would ever notice it.

Gina was looking at a series of photographs, all showing Demps in Newark, New Jersey with a tall, bosomy blonde.

"Who took these?" Gina wanted to know as she watched, her brow wrinkled, her mind unwilling to conclude what these photographs, at first blush, obviously concluded.

"A friend of mine in Newark," LaLa said. "She saw him in a restaurant there with one of those females and they seemed so chummy that she decided to snap the picture. She knew he was going to be in town on business, but this didn't seem like any business meeting to her. And when she saw him hug her as they waited for the valet to bring the car around, she decided to follow them. And she followed them right to Demps old apartment."

Gina stared at her friend. "It looks bad, okay, I'm not going to even front. But you need to talk to Demps first. After all these years he at least deserves a hearing." Gina's cell phone began to ring.

"After those pictures he doesn't deserve a damn thing."

"When is he due back in town?" Gina asked as she checked the caller ID. It was the president.

"In a couple days. But I'm thinking about going down there now."

Gina held up her finger as she answered her phone. "Hi," she said into the phone.

"Hello there," Dutch, now in the Oval Office, said. "Max tells me you had to excuse yourself from my historic presser."

"I saw your opening statement. I'm real happy for you, Dutch. And the hostages of course."

"Of course. And that press is fickle like you wouldn't believe. Yesterday I was a bumbling idiot who couldn't get anything right. Tonight, because those hostages are now safe, I'm a rock star. That's why I put zero stock in their opinions."

"I hear that."

"How's Loretta?" he asked.

Gina sighed. Looked at her friend, who looked lost, it seemed to her. "Not good," she said.

"What is it about?" Gina didn't say anything. "Dempsey?" Dutch asked.

"Bingo," Gina said. "I think I'm going to stay here tonight, Dutch. You don't need me for anything, do you?" Gina almost blushed as she listened to his answer. "Other than that," she said with a smile.

"No, I'm good. I'm going to finish up a few staff briefings and then I'm going to bed."

"What about our house guests? Don't forget about them."

"Max has already notified them that I'll see them in the morning. Give my love to Loretta. Prayerfully it'll all work out for her and Demps."

"Yes," Gina said. "I sure hope so."

"Think you need me there with you?"

"No, no, I'm good." Then Gina smiled. "Christian's here with me."

"Oh, well then," Dutch said with a smile of his own.

"Goodbye, Walter," Gina said with a grin and hung up before he could yell at her for calling him that name he hated.

"See what I'm talking about?" LaLa said to Gina as she hung up.

Gina, however, was confused. "See what?"

"You and the president. Y'all have a wonderful relationship. The best relationship I've ever seen. That's all I've ever wanted for me and Demps."

"LaLa, stop sounding so fatalistic. All you have so far are a few photos of him with some female. That's it. They aren't kissing, they aren't making love, they're just laughing and talking."

"And hugging, don't forget that."

"According to this friend of yours they were hugging. But of course she conveniently forgot to snap that telling shot. Are you sure this is a reliable friend?"

"Yes, G, she's reliable."

"What's her name?"

"Ellen Fountroy, and stop acting like some attorney. You can't explain away the evidence here."

"Look, La, I'm not saying these pictures aren't bad. They are. Especially the ones that have him going inside his apartment at night with this woman.

But the evidence is just too flimsy for you to be leaping to all kinds of conclusions just yet. You need more information. You need to talk to Demps."

"So he can deny it?" LaLa asked. "That's a brilliant plan."

Christian glanced at LaLa after her snide tone with the First Lady. But Gina didn't give it a second thought. This was a man LaLa planned to spend the rest of her life with. This was a love thing. And Gina had been around long enough to know that love can make a fool out of the most reasonable of people.

Tears began to appear in LaLa's eyes. Gina had never seen her friend so unhinged. "I thought he was in Newark on business. I thought he was there juggling family business matters. When he's there juggling females instead."

"There's hardly evidence of all of that, LaLa, let's not get it twisted."

"He wasn't like this when we were still living in Newark," LaLa said and Gina looked at her. "I never once thought of him as a cheater. But as soon as you made him your deputy press secretary, and he got a taste of power and the big time, everything changed. Now he thinks he's some mack daddy. Now he thinks he doesn't need me anymore."

LaLa began crying seriously and Gina hurried to her side.

"He doesn't need me anymore, G," LaLa cried as Gina wrapped her into her arms. "After all these years, he doesn't need me."

Gina looked at Christian, who looked as scared and pathetic as LaLa. And then she looked back at LaLa, who looked as if her world had shifted. And the responsibility Gina felt, the burden she bore, was wrenching. When she asked her friends to come and be a part of her White House staff, she never dreamed it would come to this. She remembered LaLa and Demps joking about how they were going to ride into town like conquering heroes and change that place called Washington. When, if truth be told, it was Washington that had managed to change them. And Gina, no matter how hard she tried, just couldn't divorce herself of some of that blame.

The White House residence was pin drop quiet later that night. Dutch was in bed, sound asleep, and Gina was still at LaLa's, wide awake, listening to her friend recount all of the dreams she had for a long-term relationship that now, the way LaLa saw it anyway, was near its end. She behaved as if she was mourning a death, which caused Gina to have to behave as if she was comforting the bereaved.

Back at the White House, Victoria and Caroline were also wide awake, comforting each other with their plots and schemes. Then eventually, when Victoria decided the time was right, Caroline made her way from Victoria's room and carefully opened the door and entered Dutch's.

As she moved across the floor, removed her robe and got in bed with the president, her heart was ramming against her chest. But Victoria was right.

Once he got a load of her body again, he wouldn't know what hit him. The key for her was to make certain, when he woke up, that he was already inside of her.

He was lying on his back and she had just pulled his penis out of his boxer short's opening, the side of it making her wet already, as she slid her naked body on top of him. By the time his sleepy eyes began to open, she had already commandeered his lips and was kissing him, French style.

Dutch, at first, returned her kiss, thinking, in the fog of Caroline's seduction, that it was Gina he was holding and kissing. He even began to moan, as his penis began to expand in her hand. But then he suddenly, just as she had his cock and was moving it toward her vagina, stopped. He stopped all movement.

Caroline thought it was the fact that his penis was between her legs and ready for entry that stopped him cold. But it wasn't her point of entry that had stopped him. It was her perfume. Perfume, Dutch suddenly realized, that wasn't his wife's.

His eyes flew open. When he realized that it was Caroline, not Gina, on top of him, he literally threw her off the bed, her bare backside dropping hard onto the floor. He immediately pressed his alarm button and jumped out of bed, his penis dangling out of his boxer's like some long, stiff rod. He quickly pushed it back in. But when he saw that it was Caroline pushing away from him, sliding on her butt across the floor as if she was the one under assault, his sleepy brain still couldn't quite comprehend the scene.

Victoria, who had been looking out of the cracked door of her bedroom, was horrified to see Secret Service agents materialize, seemingly out of nowhere, and hurry to the president's bedroom. She hurried there too. And there she saw Caroline, being lifted from the floor by an agent with a woman's robe being thrown around her, and her son, standing there, tying his own robe.

"What's happening here?" Victoria asked, moving further into the room. "Caroline, what's happened to you?"

Caroline was so distraught, so embarrassed, so everything that she could do nothing but cover her mouth, cry and point. Victoria looked at her son.

"Dutch," she said in her best voice of censure, "you should be ashamed of yourself!"

At first Dutch was certain he didn't hear her correctly. There was no way his mother, his own flesh and blood, was suggesting that he had orchestrated this get together. But then he realized what was happening. Caroline had gotten in his bed stark naked while he was fast asleep. Had kissed him, had fondled his penis to excitement proportions. And he was supposed to kiss his marriage, his love for Gina goodbye, just to get another taste of *her*?

These people crazy, he said inwardly, remembering a line Gina enjoyed using.

"Get out," he said out loud.

"Get out?" his mother repeated, showing pure umbrage. "How dare you throw her out? You're the one who attacked her!"

"I attacked her?" Dutch said. "Is this my room, or hers?"

Victoria had no ready answer for that one, and Dutch repeated his command. "Get out," he said again. "I want you and Caroline to get your things and get out of this house right now."

The secret service immediately began to enforce the president's order. Victoria, however, continued to take umbrage. "You're throwing *me* out?" she kept asking, astounded. "You can't throw me out!"

"Watch me, Mother," Dutch said. Then said to the agents who may have been reticent about touching his mother: "Get her out of this house and get her out now."

Caroline was still too embarrassed to fight his expulsion so she said nothing as she was grabbed by both arms and taken out of the room. Victoria, however, fought tooth and nail. It became so disturbing that she had to be manhandled, pulled out of the room as if she was a common intruder. And the entire time, as she was literally being dragged out, her small but feisty body fighting against every pull, she couldn't stop staring in disbelief at that good-for-nothing son of hers.

But she could save her shock. Just as Dutch, when his own mother came out publically against his marriage to Gina, had to save his.

When they were all gone, the woman he used to love and the mother he never knew, he slammed his bedroom door, sat on his bed, and got Gina on the phone.

FIFTEEN

By the following morning, LaLa had decided to go to Newark and "reclaim her man," as she put it, although Gina strongly advised against it, but LaLa had a one-track mind by that point. So Gina and Christian left, and both were now back at the White House. Although she had wanted to see Dutch before his day began, to eyeball him for herself and make sure he was really okay after that craziness he had to endure last night, he was already in a meeting in the Cabinet Room and therefore could not be disturbed. But when she finally did arrive at her East Wing office, a man she hadn't seen in over four years was waiting on her.

Roman stood to his feet when Gina entered the waiting area. His heart leaped with joy when he saw her again, just as it had when he had gotten her call asking for his help. She was the one that got away, that was for sure, but that was old news now. Right now he only prayed that President Harber was good to her, and that she was finding some enjoyment in her new fishbowl life.

"Hello, Wilkie," Gina said as they hugged. Roman found himself moved by her old nickname. Nobody called him that, but her.

"How are you, kid?" he asked as their hug ended and Gina stepped back. She still had that fresh, wonderful scent, still had that buoyancy he used to love about her. Still, he thought, as he glanced down, had that curvaceous, luscious bod.

"I'm good," looking at his perfectly tailored Armani suit. "What about you?"

"Fantastic."

Gina smiled. That was always his line. He'd be near death and still claim he was fantastic. "Come on back," she said and escorted him into her office. They took a seat on the office couch.

"So," he said, rubbing his big hands together, "I see our breakup didn't leave you too distraught. You've managed to do a thing or two since we last met. Got married, became First Lady of the United States of America."

Gina laughed. "Your career hasn't exactly been stagnant either, now, let's keep it real. Especially not in the female department."

Roman grinned, showing his perfect white teeth that was always so alluring to Gina against his dark-chocolaty black skin, and threw his hands up. "I plead the Fifth," he jokingly said.

"But seriously, Wilkie, I'm so glad you could make it. As I told you over the phone, I've been an attorney long enough to know all about those *I'm innocent* stories inmates love to tell. Hardly ever believe any of them, to tell you the truth. But for some reason, and maybe it as simple as the fact that we're flesh and blood, I believed Marcus Rance."

Roman nodded, sat his briefcase on the table in front of them. "You had good reason to believe him."

"Really?"

"Really," Roman said as he opened his briefcase. "There are loads of problems with his case. And I mean truckloads, Gina. This brother was so railroaded that I'm amazed the judge himself didn't criticize that jury verdict. I couldn't believe they could have come up with a guilty verdict on this case, I declare I couldn't."

"It's that open and shut?"

"Well . . . yes and no. The evidence is compelling, yes, but it's not like there's this DNA that we can point to and eliminate him as even a suspect, no. I mean, the crime was a drive-by shooting and the shots were fired from his car which, on its face, sounds very incriminating."

"Yes, it does," Gina said with a frown.

"But everything he said to you, about the job, about the stolen car, everything is true. But the witnesses his defense team called, and I mean every one of those suckers, were fatally flawed. Just horrible people. Crooks and criminals the lot of them. But," Roman continued, moving toward the edge of his seat, "they're consistent. Liars never are. They never, during that entire trial and even after the trial, changed their stories."

"But all the jury saw was the baggage."

"Exactly."

Gina stared at her friend. "Can you help him, Wilkie?"

Roman stared back, his heart sinking with the pain of what could have been if only he had realized what a diamond he had; if only he hadn't been so bent on playing the field, on bedding any woman he wanted. Now he was ready to settle down himself, to find him a woman of his own, to give up the game forever. But he was a long way from this point when he had Regina. "I'll help him," he said, "but only because you've asked me to. That brother has been an embarrassment to our race, hear what I'm saying? A disgrace! He turned it around, at least he claims he did, but that still doesn't mean he wasn't a terror before he turned it around."

"I hear you, Wilkie."

"But for you, I'll help. Because you know I'll do anything for you."

Gina nodded, because, back in the day, he would have. He just couldn't seem to be faithful to her, which kind of sealed their fate as a couple. "Thanks," she said. "Now show me what you've got."

Roman smiled as he pulled papers from his briefcase and laid them out on the table. He used to show her what he had every night; used to show it to her repeatedly. And he missed that. He missed the way she made him feel. He missed her honesty and integrity. He missed her, yes, he'd admit it. He missed her deeply.

But they didn't call him a lawyer's lawyer for nothing. He got down to the business at hand.

Dutch and Max left the Cabinet Room after a contentious meeting with the principals about the hit on Gina's convoy, and headed for Gina's office on the

East Wing. But the topic of conversation wasn't the convoy hit, or the hostages' success, or Roman Wilkes and their Marcus Rance problem. They were discussing that craziness the night before.

"What are the options?" Dutch asked his chief of staff.

"Your mother could go back to Nantucket and vow never to speak to you again, keeping quiet about what happened because of the embarrassment it could cause her. Or," Max continued, praying that the former would be the case, "she could get loud."

"And do what?"

"I don't know, Dutch. You know her better than anybody on the face of this earth--"

"Which is saying absolutely nothing. After I took Regina to see her and she showed me what she was really made of, I don't think I know that woman at all. And after last night, I don't think I ever did."

"She's something else, Dutch, you'd better believe that. She plays it from angles we wouldn't even think about playing it from. That's why Harber Industries became the successful company it became. Not because of your father. He was a bit of a cad in the long run, a lovable, sweet man, but a cad. It was your mother's hard hand and determination that kept that company in the big leagues. Don't underestimate her, is all I can say."

"And Caroline?" Dutch asked, his heart a little less settled regarding her.

"Our Caroline problem is a little trickier," Max said as the two men got onto the elevator. "If she sticks with Victoria, she could spell serious trouble. You know, selling her story to the tabloids to make a little money, sitting around on couches on TV talk shows telling about all of the pressure you put her under before the wedding and that's why she disappeared. But if she decides the gig is up, her seduction scheme didn't work, and she packs up and sails her ass back to France, I'll sigh relief."

"Amen," Dutch said, as they stepped off of the elevator.

Max looked at him. "You still love her, don't you?"

Dutch shook his head. "I do not. Not after that kind of betrayal. She knew how I felt about her, but she decided to pretend she was dead because she felt pressured? I'm not buying that, Max. She knew I would have called off that wedding in a heartbeat if she didn't want it. But she just takes off and stays off? No. I can't love a woman like that. You don't treat somebody you love that way."

He said this and then headed into the office of the First Lady. And it was Max's time to say amen.

Dutch's first impression of Roman Wilkes, seeing him sitting there on that couch next to his wife, was how powerfully built he appeared in person. On television he had a command presence about him, but nothing like this. Roman Wilkes had the look of a man who could have anything, and any woman he wanted. And one of his primary wants, it seemed to Dutch, appeared to be Regina.

That was Dutch's initial impression anyway when he and Max walked into his wife's office and saw the two of them sitting there. Before them were stacks of papers and file folders, but the man's big, bright eyes seemed to be focused rather exclusively on Gina.

When Roman saw who had entered the room, however, he quickly diverted his now lust-filled eyes, and stood to his feet. "Mr. President," he said, extending his hand. "It's an honor to meet you, sir."

"The honor is all mine," Dutch said, shaking his hand. "This is Maxwell Brennan, my chief of staff."

"Yes, of course," Roman said, shaking Max's hand. "Mr. Brennan."

"Have a seat, please," Dutch insisted and Roman sat back down. "I understand my wife has sought your legal expertise."

"Yes, sir, and on a dogged case I must say."

"Hello honey," Dutch said, as he leaned over and kissed Gina on the lips. She had spent the night away from him, and he missed her dearly. Tonight, when he had her in his bed, he was going to show her just how much. He took a seat in the chair flanking the couch. Max stood beside his chair. "What's the verdict?"

Gina looked at Roman. "What's the verdict, Wilkie?" she asked her friend.

"If I had to render it based on what I've uncovered," Roman said, "I would say one hundred percent not guilty."

This astonished Dutch. Roman was known as a lot of things, a ladies man topping the list, but he was also known as an excellent attorney. His conclusions carried weight. "Are you saying," Dutch said, attempting to not even think about the implications, "that our criminal justice system got it wrong? That we imprisoned an innocent man?"

"Hardly," Max, the forever skeptic, said.

"Oh, I wouldn't dismiss it at all, Mr. Brennan," Roman said. "I would bet my practice that Marcus Rance did not commit those murders. Everything that was used against him at his trial can be disproved. From the fact that he did, in fact, report his car stolen some weeks before that drive by shooting, to the fact that he did clock-in at work, he did have the company truck, and he was on time with all of his deliveries that day. His partner on the delivery truck testified that he was working with him that day, and is willing to testify to that fact again."

"But he already testified to that fact, right?" Max said. "Which means the jury didn't believe his testimony."

"Because he was a convicted felon, yes, sir."

"That's not the reason. Why would you say that's the reason?"

"Because it happens," Roman said, staring at Max. "You do know that. Right?"

Max was offended, both Dutch and Gina could tell. "The point is," Max said, "what do you propose that we do with this new twist on that old evidence?"

Roman glanced at Gina, as if he couldn't believe this guy. "I will have to make this old evidence appear as shiny brand new as humanly possible, first of all, to even file a subsequent petition for a writ of habeas corpus. Or, I will have to try to petition the court under the Brady exception, which means I would have to prove that the prosecution knew some relevant information, such as the fact that he did indeed report his car as stolen but they suppressed that information at trial. Short of those two limited exceptions, we have nothing the courts will hear. Especially those courts in Texas. But once we get it all in a neat little package, and because it's Texas we'd better put a bow on top, then we'll enter a motion to vacate, or to set aside the judgment."

"Are you kidding me?" Max asked. "This isn't some social club you're sitting in. This is the White House. This is Dutch Harber's presidency, his legacy. We can't tarnish it with some rehashed, so-called new evidence that exonerates his brother-in-law. The public will go ballistic if that happens. They already believe that commutation of his death sentence was favoritism. This would be a whole other ballgame."

"I understand that," Roman said.

"Well I'm thrilled you understand it, Mr. Wilkes, because we can't have that."

"You can't have it? But, Mr. Brennan, I don't think *you* understand. We're talking about a man's life here."

When Max still seemed stuck on stupid, as Roman thought of him, he and Gina looked to Dutch. Dutch stood to his feet, causing Roman to stand, too. Dutch placed both hands in his pant pockets. "Do whatever you need to do to uncover the truth," he said to Roman. "Consider yourself retained by me."

"Dutch!" Max decried.

Dutch frowned and looked at him. "What?"

"Are you. . .," Max started, remembered who he was talking to, and tried to calm back down. "Sir, you can't be a part of this. You have to think about the mid-terms. You won't be running, but what about the rest of us?"

Gina looked up at Max. Dutch was already staring at him. "What about the rest of whom, Max? Who are us?"

Max glanced over and Roman and Gina. "May we talk about this privately, sir?"

"Are you considering public office, Max?"

Max hesitated. "I've considered it, yes."

"Which office?"

"I haven't decided yet."

He was lying, and Dutch knew it. Why he was lying, however, was probably the bigger story. Sometimes Dutch wondered if there was any human being on the face of this earth, besides his wife, that he could truly trust. He looked at Roman. "I pray I never become the kind of human being who will allow an innocent man to rot in prison because it may not look good politically for me. As I stated earlier, consider yourself retained. By me."

Roman extended his hand. "I know the political costs for you, sir. I assure you I'll handle it with the utmost discretion. Thank-you."

"And take advice from the First Lady," Dutch added as he shook Roman's hand, although he wasn't at all sure that he wanted this good looking fellow to spend another second with his wife. "She's an excellent attorney in her own right."

"Oh, don't you worry about that, sir," Roman said, smiling down at Gina. "I plan to use the mess out of her."

That line didn't particularly sit well with Dutch, as Gina grinned at her old friend and, Dutch thought, her old lover, but he had a meeting to get to. He and Max left, with Max saying nothing more about his own political ambitions.

That night in bed, Gina lay naked on her stomach while her husband's big bulk lay on top of her, his penis deep inside of her, moving in a slow motion, sensual rhythm, as Dutch was determined to remove all thoughts of Roman Wilkes from her mind. He never told her that was his intention, but as he made love to her, they both knew that was exactly what was going on.

Gina closed her eyes as her body heated feverishly to that wonderfully relaxing feel of his entrance. His hands cupped her breasts, squeezing them every time he swiped her g-spot, making her groan with wonderment at how he could be so certain of his target and hit it over and over again. And he kept swiping her, at just the right angle, in just the right spot, as he slid in a sweet drag that rubbed her walls to a wet sensual high that she never wanted to end. She knew the man was tired, she knew it had been yet another long behind day, but she wanted him to keep fucking her exactly the way he was doing it. Rubbing her walls, hitting her spot, saturating her with his wet, perfect, harmonious love.

Dutch closed his eyes as he fucked her, as he felt the harmony too. His hardened thighs rubbed against her tight ass as his penis stayed lodged inside of her and danced an enormously gratifying slow drag with her g-spot. He kept thrusting against her walls, moving deeper and deeper inside of her, hearing the slapping sounds of his penis sloshing around her wetness until it engorged and his entire body tightened, stiffened, and then released its own juices. A release that caused Gina to cry out, as she reached the summit too.

Afterwards, as they lay in each other's arms, both gratified in knowing that nobody was going to take away their love, Gina looked at Dutch.

"Heard from your mother?"

"I have not."

"So Caroline made her little move while the cat was away."

Dutch snorted. "She certainly tried to."

"Egged-on by your mother, no doubt."

"Of course. When I was engaged to Caroline, she could hardly stand her. Now they're best friends? I don't believe it." Then he pulled Gina in his arms, his eyes once again showing sensuality and staring at her lips. "But the good news," he said, "is that they have gone back to their bat caves and will leave us alone."

"Yes," Gina said, as they kissed on the lips. They were gone all right, she thought as he moved her on top of him, still kissing her, but she had an awfully hard time believing that they had gone in peace, never to be heard from again.

SIXTEEN

Caroline arrived downstairs just as Nathan Riles was escorting Max Brennan out of Victoria's front door. More than a little curious since Max was usually acting on behalf of Dutch, she hurried to the morning room where she expected to find her benefactor.

"What was Max doing here?" she asked the president's mother.

Victoria, who was seated at a small tea table, sipped her tea. "Business. As in none of yours."

That bitch, Caroline thought. "Any word from Dutch?" she asked.

"None. It's as if he thinks he can dismiss us out of hand. With no retribution."

Caroline looked at Victoria. "Will there be retribution?"

Victoria smirked, sipped her tea. "What do you think?"

"I think you should pay me my money and let me be on my way. Dutch doesn't want me. You should have seen the way he looked at me when he realized I was the one on top of him, kissing him, and not that wife of his."

"It beggars understanding," Victoria said, mystified. "What on earth could he see in that woman?"

"Whatever it is, he's not seeing it in me." Then Caroline's bitterness began to show. "If you would have left well enough alone," she added, "I would be his wife today, you would have had boatloads of light-skinned grand kids, and there would be no issues at all. Instead, you force me out of his life and get stuck with the daughter-in-law from the black lagoon."

"She's no in-law of mine," Victoria said as the door of the morning room opened.

"Your guest has arrived, ma'am," Nathan Riles said.

"Thank-you, Nathan," Victoria said as she stood to her feet. "You let me handle this," she said to Caroline. "Any talk of getting paid is far too premature. You're still on the clock-remember that. I'll not pay a dime unless you perform to my satisfaction."

"And does that mean my getting back with Dutch, which is an impossibility and we both know it?"

"After what he did to me, the way he treated me, I don't give a rat's ass who he's with. It's his destruction I want, not his happiness. Not anymore. Not after what he did to me."

Victoria gave her a hard look, her cold blue eyes devoid of any hint of warmth, and then she walked out of the room.

And walked around two corridors to her parlor. Waiting for her in the parlor was yet another one of Dutch's females.

"Kate, darling," she said as she entered the room, "how are you?"

Kate Marris turned around. Stared Victoria in those cold blue eyes. Making clear by her look alone that this had better be as profitable as Victoria claimed it would be, or she would live to regret it. "Fine," she said. "And you?"

The presidential motorcade was treated to cheers and applause when it arrived in Bethesda at Walter Reed. The rescued hostages would be treated there before they would be released to their respective families, and the president and First Lady had agreed to meet their plane. From the press to the military brass to families of the hostages and regular citizens, everybody wanted in on the excitement.

Dutch and Gina, LaLa and Christian rode in the president's car, and they all were amazed at the turnout.

"They really love you, sir," Christian said, looking out the window at the throngs of people.

"Don't you believe it," Dutch said, looking out of the window too. "It's a momentary condition called short memory. As soon as the hoopla is over, they'll remember 'oh, yeah, I hate his guts,' and get back to it." Christian and Gina laughed. "It's the name of the Washington game."

Gina looked at LaLa, who looked barely there. She went to Newark to confront Demps, who was still there. She had expected him to deny everything, to declare that she was completely mistaken, that he hasn't looked at any other woman that way in all the years they've been together, that he wouldn't think about fooling around with another woman. Instead, she got a man who didn't deny a thing. "Yeah, I did it," LaLa had said he said, "so what?"

Of course Gina knew he wasn't as bold as that, but the end result was the same: he didn't want LaLa anymore. And that, Gina thought as she looked at her friend, was what hurt LaLa the most. The fact that he was so over her, so easily out of love after nearly a decade of love. Or at least what LaLa thought was love. Gina thought it was love too, until she moved the two of them to Washington and they both got a taste of life on the biggest stage of all. Women wanted to be close to that power and in Demps they saw a way to get there. Men saw it too, and tried to get next to LaLa. But LaLa wasn't thinking about those brothers. Gina could see that Demps, however, loved the attention of those grand, supermodel-type women who, before his appointment as her deputy press secretary, wouldn't have given a man like him the time of day, and he wasn't so easily dismissive.

"You could have taken the day off, La," she said to her friend.

"I told her," Christian said.

"I know, but I prefer to work. Besides, we have a victory. It's a rare thing nowadays. I wanted to be a part of it."

Dutch squeezed Gina's hand. He had been betting on Loretta and Dempsey, was certain they would go the distance. But they get to Washington and start falling apart. The cracks had to have already been there, he knew something like that didn't just happen, but if they would have stayed in Newark perhaps those cracks would have had a chance to mend.

"He called me," Gina said, and LaLa looked at her. And that hopefulness in LaLa's eyes, as if she wanted his conversation to have been all about his love for her, broke Gina's heart.

"What did he want?" LaLa asked her.

"Reassurance from me that his job as my deputy press secretary was safe."

"That asshole!" Christian said, and then, when everybody looked at him in surprise, caught himself. "Excuse me, ma'am, and Mr. President, and excuse me, LaLa." They all, even LaLa, laughed. "But the nerve of him. He didn't ask about LaLa, or talk about their relationship, he just wanted to know about his job? He doesn't deserve you, La. I'm sorry but he doesn't."

"No man does if we left it up to you, Chris," Dutch said and Gina looked at him. Then back at Christian. She suspected that he might have some kind of innocent crush on LaLa, but dang. She had no idea he had discussed that crush with Dutch.

"But anyway," Gina said, "that's all he wanted to discuss, girl. Keeping his job and nothing else." She wanted LaLa to bury any illusions she still had about Demps coming around. He may come around, but she didn't want her friend banking on it.

"So what did you tell him?" LaLa asked.

"What you think? I told him he was fired." LaLa smiled. "Nobody's breaking my best friend's heart and I welcome him back with open arms. I mean, come on. He was my deputy press-sec. He gets hired and keeps his job at the pleasure of the First Lady. I told him I no longer have pleasure in keeping him around. And he actually was surprised by that, got all hot with me. You should have heard him. I told him no need to be getting upset with me. He's the one who messed up. He's the one who decided to break your heart. What did he expect me to do? Working in the White House isn't like working in any ordinary business. I have to have people around me I can trust. How can I trust him if even the woman he had purported to love can't? I mean honestly?" Then Gina shook her head. "He has really changed."

"He hadn't changed all that much," LaLa said and both Dutch and Gina looked at him.

"You mean you've had trouble like this before?"

LaLa nodded with a frown.

Gina could hardly believe it. "Why didn't you tell me, La? I told you everything." She glanced at Dutch. "Almost everything."

"I know, but I didn't want you or anybody else to get the wrong impression of Demps. I mean, yeah, I've had my suspicions in the past, but he would deny it all so I believed him. Or at least I wanted to believe him. But when he got to Washington and got a look at some of the most desirable women in the world, and these women were paying attention to him, he just took it to a whole different level. Great looking men were doing me the same way, so I can relate. But what Demps didn't seem to understand was that those women and those men weren't seeing us, they were seeing our proximity to power; they were seeing our positions. But he just knew it was him. When I found out he had taken one of those *desirable* women with him on his trip back home, I just flipped and had to see it for myself. And then, when I got there, and saw this woman in his apartment, saw this woman all hugged up with him, he treated me like I was the intruder. Not the other woman, but me." Tears tried to well in LaLa's eyes, but she forced them to stay at bay. "It just hurts, you know?"

Christian immediately slid closer to her, and put his arm around her. "You'll weather this storm too, LaLa," he said.

"And then he called me," Dutch said and all three looked at him.

"What did he say?" LaLa asked, that hopeful look returning to her eyes.

"He wanted to know if I would intervene on his behalf to get his job back." LaLa deflated again. "I told him," Dutch continued, "that whatever my wife had already relayed to him, he should go with that."

LaLa smiled. "Oh, I'll bet he loved that."

"No more than he deserves," Dutch said and they all laughed, although Gina could still see that hurt in her friend's eyes.

Then the limo crawled to a stop, the doors were opened by the secret service, and Dutch and Gina stepped out to the roar of the crowd.

"It's show time," Dutch said, buttoning his suit coat. "Let's smile like the circus acts they take us for, and lay it on thick."

Gina smiled, but more at Dutch's joke than the roaring crowds. She knew all about those roaring crowds. Because Dutch had it right. Today he was their conquering hero. Tomorrow their goat.

Dutch pressed his hand into the small of her back and ushered her to their, at least for right now, adoring public.

Christian pressed his hand into the small of LaLa's back, which immediately released that lonely, depressing feeling, as they followed much further behind.

It was a calm morning and Victoria Harber decided to sit lakeside on her estate. The fact that Roman Wilkes, famed criminal defense attorney and the man Max had told her was an ex-lover of the First Lady's, was her guest that morning had everything to do with her decision. She was no outdoors type. She rarely walked the grounds of her own estate. But she wanted him to understand that she was no nouveau riche who, like him, had to continue working to keep the money growing. It had already grown. She was already there.

Roman looked at the briefcase on his lap that was filled with half a million dollars. Then he looked at her, still astounded that he was actually making this kind of transaction with the mother of the President of the United States.

"No-one knows?" he asked this, staring as if studying her. She had the coldest eyes he'd ever seen.

"No-one," she assured him. "You get that five hundred thousand now, and then another five hundred thousand when the photos appear."

Roman looked at the money again. He would have to take on a lot of cases, over long stretches of time, to earn this much dough. "This is a lot of money," he said.

"I'm aware of that," Victoria said.

"A lot of money to throw away."

"If you produce the kind of photos I am talking about, it won't be thrown anywhere. It will, in fact, be the best investment I could have ever made."

Roman studied her. "You really hate the First Lady that much?"

"I don't hate her at all. I don't know her to hate her. My son has seen to that. But you're a smart man, Mr. Wilkes. That's why my people gave you a call. It's my understanding that you know how to handle jobs and keep it all very discreet. This isn't about my love, or hate, or more likely, indifference towards the First La . . ., towards that woman. It is, however, about creating an image around that woman."

"And your son?" Roman added.

"Yes, and my son," Victoria admitted.

Roman exhaled. "So you want me to photograph myself hugging and kissing the First Lady?"

"Exactly," Victoria said.

"And how do you propose I do such a thing?"

"She's given you White House clearance as her personal attorney."

"Now how would you know about such a confidential matter?"

"I know everything that goes on in that house of ill repute."

Roman smiled. "House of Ill-repute? Is that what the White House is nowadays?"

"That's exactly what it is."

Roman stared at her. "Now I know you, Mrs. Harber. I've heard nothing but glowing testimonies about your charitable work on behalf of the poor and downtrodden. So I just know this characterization of yours has absolutely nothing to do with the fact that a sister is currently occupying that White House. Nothing whatsoever."

"Nothing whatsoever," Victoria repeated, her eyes revealing nothing.

Roman smiled. "I'll get your photographs," he said.

"And then get them published, remember that."

"Of course."

"I don't want you simply hugging her," Victoria warned. "That won't be enough for that second payment. I need you kissing her on those big lips of hers." Roman looked at her. "I need her perhaps on your lap or something."

213

"I can hug her. Can even get away with an innocent, chaste kiss that those photos, in the hands of some malicious journalist, just might interpret as anything but chaste and innocent. But the lap thing ain't gonna happen. Not with Regina Lansing. She's doesn't roll like that."

"Well," Victoria said, finding the entire situation deplorable, "I don't care how she rolls." Roman laughed. "I just want those photos published. And when the public, a public, I might add, that generally detests her anyway, finds that she's been less than this stellar woman my son is just so certain she is, your work will have been done. And you'll get your second payment. But those photos had better be convincing."

"No problem," Roman said, relishing this infusion of cash. "I never turn down an opportunity to earn real money."

"She's not a bad looking woman," Victoria said with a deceptive smile. "You're a ladies man, it's obvious. You'll probably enjoy yourself."

"No doubt," Roman said, now looking at her. "And you're right, she is a good looking woman. But even so," he added, "she's got nothing on you."

Victoria found herself blushing. Why the ideal of it! *Him* flirting with *her*? Absurd! She looked at the peaceful lake, opting to ignore his flirtation.

Roman smiled and looked back down at that money. Half a mil on his lap.

As he looked at his ill-gotten gain, however, Victoria took another look at him. And at his big, black, rock solid she was certain, muscular body.

SEVENTEEN

The weeks came and went and the State Dinner in honor of the president of Russia was going right along without a hitch. Gina was already being praised in the press for her gown choice, Dutch was still riding high in the polls because of the hostage rescue, and the White House State Room was abuzz with energy and that relaxed happiness Dutch and Gina had rarely enjoyed. All, it seemed to Gina, was right with the world.

Which probably meant, she also knew, that something was up.

It wasn't a reality, however, until later that night. Dutch was laughing with the Russian president about something the German Chancellor had said, when Max walked across the room and whispered something in the president's ear. Gina was seated further away, listening to the First Lady of France go on and on about her former modeling career, when Dutch excused himself, stood and left the room. For some reason, Gina's heart began to pound. She searched out LaLa and Christian. When Christian saw her, he leaned over to LaLa.

"It's the beauty of the thing," he said, which was the code to be used when the First Lady needed an exit strategy.

LaLa immediately rose, whispered the same line in Gina's ear, and Gina excused herself and also left the room.

"Where is he?" she asked Allison, who was standing in the Cross Hall. "The Oval?"

"Max's office," Allison said, and Gina headed in that direction.

When she entered the room, she saw Max on one side of the president and the White House Counsel on the other side of him. The two men flanking Dutch had such a defensive stance that it almost looked to Gina as if Dutch was under some sort of attack and they were his bodyguards. Also in the room were the Attorney General and the president's National Security Advisor. They were all staring at the television. Gina looked too.

It was, as it usually was when bad news was about to break, a press conference. Victoria Harber was at the podium, surrounded by Jennifer Caswell, Caroline Parker, and Kate Marris. Kate Marris, Gina thought. They dragged her out too? She was one of the president's ex's who had accused him of impregnating her, only to suffer a miscarriage. Now she was standing on the stage too. And the only thing she seemed to have in common with the other three females behind Victoria was that she, too, was once Dutch's woman.

But that wasn't the real surprise. The real surprise wasn't their joint appearance, but what was said during their appearance.

Dutch, all three ladies were now claiming, raped them.

The reporters, and rightly so, at first seemed skeptical. Especially since one of the women, Jennifer Caswell, had recently withdrawn her accusation of rape. But she had a ready answer for their skepticism.

"The White House pressured me into recanting," she said, "with threats of exposing my husband's business problems. As some of you may know, it's no secret that a few of Ralph's competitors used to accuse him of being involved in unsavory practices. Some have accused him of earning his billions because of those practices. I know it's not true, but the White House had guaranteed that the Feds would find that it was true and that his good name would be forever sullied. And every dime of his money could be seized."

"What nonsense!" the Attorney General bellowed.

"I felt such pressure," Jennifer continued. "I didn't want his name sullied."

"Nor his billions seized," Max pointed out.

"But what was a girl to do?" Jennifer asked as if she was some blonde air-head rather than the tough, smart, force of nature she truly was.

And the reporters pointed out the nonsensicalness of her allegations. And then Kate stepped up, declaring that Dutch used to force himself on her "on numerous occasions." When a reporter, rightly, pointed out that she never mentioned it before, even when she was accusing him, during her pregnancy, of being a deadbeat dad, she, too, had her answer ready.

"I loved him so much," she declared, "that I couldn't hurt him that way. I thought that he would come to his senses and come back to me. Then after he married that woman, who I still believe is out to destroy and divide this country, I was so distraught I couldn't even think straight. But when I saw Jennifer on television telling her story, and then being forced to recant it, I knew I had to eventually come forward too."

"What a load of bullocks!" the White House Counsel said. "You raped her on numerous occasions, yet she wanted you back? If you don't sue the pants off of these bimbos, Mr. President, I will," he declared.

Then it was Caroline's time to stand at the podium. Dutch's heart began to hammer when she stood there. Gina looked at him. Of all the women on that stage, she knew that he once really loved Caroline.

But she showed him no mercy, either. He not only raped her, she declared, but she had the film footage to prove it.

Then they cued up the camera, dimmed the lights and lit up the screen. On that screen was indeed the president's bedroom. On that screen was Dutch in bed, with a naked Caroline, who didn't even bother to obscure her nakedness, kissing Dutch and rubbing her bare backside against his midsection. And then suddenly a different video appeared of the Lincoln Monument, as if it had been accidentally recorded over. Then the tape returned to the bedroom scene, but by now Caroline was on the floor, backing up on her ass, with Dutch just standing there, as if she was terrified and trying to get away from him. Then, of course, the tape was interrupted again with more footage of sights around the National Mall.

The tape itself would undoubtedly be lost completely by the time Dutch's attorneys could get the necessary injunction so that their experts can check it for any doctoring, including any recording over, accidental or otherwise. But the damage was clearly already done.

And the White House Counsel said it best:

"One woman, two women, even three women, yes, we could have fought each and every one of their assertions," he said, his eyes never leaving the television screen. "It would have been difficult to sway that court of public opinion, don't get me wrong. Especially with your own mother leading the charge. But we could have at least made a valiant effort. But a tape showing the president actually kissing, actually in bed with a naked woman? And this woman skirting away from him as if he had just done something terrible to her? How in the world," he asked, his own face now a mask of concern, "are we going to counter that?"

Gina looked at her husband, tears already in her eyes. He walked away from the TV, rubbing his forehead, his once proud body now sagged by the weight of his own discontent. And he stood at the office window, his back to them all, as he tried with all he had to look beyond the clutter, the congestion, the pain of Washington DC, and see the long view.

That press conference was so devastating that it tore through the roof in Washington and became the scandal of scandals, not just in the backyards and at the kitchen tables of middle America, but around the world, with that video providing the proof they all needed that Dutch Harber, the gorgeous, affable President of the United States, the well-respected leader of the free world, just might be a monster.

Congress was the first to jump on the *slay the monster* bandwagon when, later the next day, the Democratic Speaker of the House and the Republican Senate Majority Leader issued a joint statement demanding that the president either resign, or face articles of impeachment.

By the time their statement reached the White House press office, Allison Shearer was about ready to explode. Her office was packed with staffers, every one of them on their cell phones and BlackBerrys, but her voice carried over every one.

"You know Dutch Harber!" she yelled into the phone, yelled even though she was talking to the Speaker of the House. "You know he could never rape anyone! That tape's been doctored and you know it. Once we get a hold of it and expose the truth, Jed, you're going to wish you never made that statement. Resign or face impeachment. Seriously?

Impeachment based on the lies of desperate women? How could you betray the president like that?"

But the Speaker held to his guns. That video speaks for itself, he said, and hung up the phone.

Allison hung up too, but then got angrier just thinking about his arrogance. She then picked the phone back up, ready to remind that Speaker that all of those hefty donations he was relying on for his upcoming reelection campaign had to be approved for release by the DNC, which, she reminded him, was under the president's control. But then Max entered her office. With a stack of newspapers of his own showing the headlines from around the world. And if she thought the Speaker was harsh, his face seemed to say, wait until you get a load of these.

He dropped them on her desk.

Allison, seeing that look on Max's face, put the phone back down. And cleared her office.

Max slouched down in the chair in front of her. "I can't believe it, Ally," he said. "This story just broke and already the president has become the joke of the world. Even the French government is insisting that he apologizes to Caroline Parker."

"The French?"

"Because she lived in France for that decade she was in hiding."

Allison shook her head. "That is so bogus."

"I know. But they don't even question that decade-old absence of hers. All they see is that video."

The door opened, and LaLa peered inside. "Hello, Ally," she said. Allison motioned her to come in. She did, with Christian coming in with her.

"What's up, LaLa?" Allison asked.

"I was about to ask you the same thing."

Allison shook her head. "Max was just telling me how that video reigns supreme around the world."

"Isn't it awful?" Christian said. "The president and First Lady are still reeling from it all."

Max looked at him. "You've seen the president?"

"No, sir. We haven't seen either one of them. But I'm just saying. They have to be reeling."

"He won't see me," Max said.

Allison looked at him. "Why not?"

Max hunched his shoulders, although he had a pretty good idea why. Dutch had been treating him differently ever since he had to reveal he was secretly planning a run for office. Max wouldn't put it past him if he suspected he was in cahoots with his mother. Which he was, but not to bring Dutch down, he'd never do that. But to bring that wife of his down. She was Dutch's problem and the sooner he realized it, Max thought, the better.

"What's the deal with that video tape anyway?" LaLa asked. "Was the Counsel's office able to get an injunction?"

"They got it," Allison said, "but the video has mysteriously disappeared. Nobody knows what's happened to it."

"Are you serious?"

"Oh, yes, I'm very serious," Allison said, looking down at the newspapers. "When you're rich and powerful like Victoria Harber you can get away with craziness like that." When Allison saw some of the headlines, her disgust with the media tripled. "Oh my goodness, these people!" she yelled.

"What?" Christian asked.

Allison began to read the headlines: "'President Harber: The *Can't Get Enough of Your Love* President.' Then this: 'Could This President Be Your Baby's daddy?'"

LaLa shook her head.

"And get a load of this: 'She said it was long, thick, and juicy.'"

"How can they write this dribble?" Christian wanted to know.

"And this," Allison said, still reading headlines: "'Dutch Harber: President Ding Dong. The President who did black, and went back.'"

"It's outrageous," Christian said.

"You think that's bad," Max said. "There's no less than seven investigations looking into their ridiculous allegations, including the FBI, the Secret Service, the Capitol Police because Kate Marris claims one of the rapes occurred while Dutch was a member of the Senate, the DC Police, and even the French Police in case some of the assaults occurred on French soil while Caroline was living there."

"Oh, so he supposedly hopped a plane to France and raped her there too?" LaLa asked.

"They all want in on the freak show, La, what can I say?" Max said.

"And don't forget all of those Congressional Hearings their scheduling as we speak," Allison said. "Every subcommittee known to man wants to drag the president's cabinet before them to find out what did they know and when did they know it. They're treating this crap like some gotdamn Watergate!"

"This is so unfair!"

"You're telling me?" Allison said. "I have to call them out on their unfairness and they just laugh in my face. They have this president exactly where they want him and they are not about to let him up because of anything as foreign to them as fairness."

LaLa exhaled, she could just imagine what Dutch and Gina were going through. "What can we do to stop the hemorrhaging?" she asked Allison.

"Absolutely nothing," Allison replied. "That's the scary part. It will take Divine intervention to turn this disaster around."

LaLa, a true believer in Divine intervention, silently began to pray for exactly that.

Gina found Dutch out on the Truman Balcony later that next day. He had spent half of the night huddling with his staff and legal advisors and when he ultimately retired to bed he opted to sleep, as Gina had expected, in the guest bedroom. She started to give him his space, to allow him a chance to decompress without her having to see him worried to death over the burdens a president bore.

But she just couldn't do it this time. Because this was not a burden outside of himself. This wasn't about hostages or economic downturns or natural disasters. This was about him and his character. And that burden belonged to her.

That was why, last night, she went to the guest bedroom. To her surprise, he was not even in bed, but was crotched down in a corner leaned against the wall, a drink in his hand, his head dropped down. He was so spooked by the turn of events that he was not even aware that someone had entered the room.

Gina just stood there watching him. Why do they always seek to destroy the good guys, she wondered, when the crooks and selfish pigs were allowed to operate with reckless abandon and nobody cared? But a man like Dutch Harber, a man good to his core, gets raked over the coals like it was nobody's business. Day in and day out. From one craziness to another craziness. All in the name of challenging the government, of making sure the leaders did not get ahead of themselves and drunk with power. And once they have him cowering in a corner, they're happy. Their work has been done. And they can crawl back under the rocks they crawled out of and leave that broken man for her to put back together.

When they knew, like she knew, that a vessel forced to be glued back together was never the same.

She crotched down in front of him, her eyes now narrowed and showing that look of earnestness that he knew so well. At this point she knew he knew she was there, but it took him a while to acknowledge that presence. And when he did look up, the pain in his bewildered green eyes was palpable.

And when tears began to drain from those eyes, all of the words Gina had planned to speak, all of the reassurances she had planned to make, became caught in her throat. And suddenly there was nothing, nothing at all, that she could say.

She, instead, moved over to him and pulled him into her arms.

That was last night. But now, in the light of day, when she found him seated in a chair on the Truman Balcony, staring out across the peaceful South Lawn, he still had the look of a person in the throes of trauma.

She sat next to him in a flanking chair.

"Good morning," she said.

He smiled at her, and it was a smile laced with pain, but she knew, under the circumstances, it was the best that he could do. "Good morning."

"I see your staff canceled all of your appearances too."

"Yes, they did," he said. "I was supposed to address a local elementary school about our educational initiatives. It was supposed to be the launch of our counter to the No Child Left Behind bill. But given the circumstances, they didn't think it would be appropriate."

Dutch seemed to wince with pain after he said that, and he looked back out over the lawn. The idea that they would think he was such a moral deviant that he couldn't be around kids angered Gina. But he didn't need her negative energy too.

So they just sat there, quietly, for what seemed like hours, but was actually a matter of minutes.

"I had planned to take you to lunch today," he finally said. "Over at that new restaurant on Capitol Hill, but under the circumstances . . ."

"Is that the new normal for us, Dutch? Our life will have to cease because everything we planned to do will fall within that *under the circumstances* or *because of the circumstances* or *given the circumstances* qualifier?"

"It does seem rather confining, doesn't it?"

"It seems downright wrong," Gina couldn't help but say.

Dutch snorted. "We have measured out our lives," Dutch said, quoting T.S. Eliot, "in coffee spoons."

"And in short," Gina added, quoting Eliot too, "I was afraid."

Dutch's heart rammed against his chest and he looked at his wife. He was so sorry that she had to go through this; so sorry that he didn't drop out of that reelection race when he had the chance, and had let the hounds of hell have this.

Now she was afraid.

And so was he.

He took her hand.

"You know the one thing that perhaps hurt more than anything else?" he said.

There's *one* thing, Gina thought, when there was so much to choose from? "What?" she asked.

"The fact that my own mother orchestrated this whole thing because she wanted to break up my marriage. And she played to the peanut gallery. Played to the haters and doubters. What self-respecting woman, was her logic, would remain with a man like me, an accused monster on videotape? And she didn't want our marriage to end because she didn't think you were good enough for me. That train of thought would have been too much like normal. But no, she wanted to break us up because she didn't think you were good enough for *her*. And her precious, lily white-or so she chooses to believe, bloodline. She wants our marriage to end before we give to her, before we put in her bloodline, a grandchild that could possibly be closer to your skin color than mine."

"And she assumed you would wait, that you wouldn't want to raise a child in this environment."

"Right."

Gina, however, wrinkled her brow. "But I still don't understand," she said. "If it's all about race, why would she want you to be with Caroline? I thought you said Caroline was rumored to be half-black herself."

"Oh, she is half-black. It was more than just rumor. But that's the madness of racism. Because it isn't about real truth. It's about perceived truth. And my mother doesn't believe for a second that a woman who looks as white as Caroline and carries herself the way she carries herself could possibly be anything but white. She knows better, but she's pretended so long that she doesn't, until she really doesn't."

Dutch hesitated. He used to idolize his mother for all of her wonderful, charitable work. Now he had to fight not to hate her. "My mother has spent her entire privileged life around poor, destitute blacks and black servants, and she felt good about herself because she was always the one on top, always the one in position to help the less fortunate among us. When she runs into a smart, savvy, sharp African-American, she's certain there's something wrong with them too. Because they don't fit into the box. Because they upset her manufactured truth. Because her sense of superiority is challenged when she sees superior blacks too. That's why the least little thing you do, she pounces. You wear an African-style outfit, or calls a reporter a fool, it all plays into her nice little narrative that says you aren't one of us, you're different, you're that *other*."

Dutch shook his head, disgusted. "Thank God people like my mother are fast becoming a dying breed."

Gina nodded, although they weren't dying fast enough for her liking. "So she champions a half-black woman like Caroline in order to stop an all-black woman like me?"

"Right, although nobody's all-white, nobody's all-black. Nothing's black and white, cut and dry like that anymore. But it is in my mother's mind. So she sees Caroline as all-white because she has to see her that way. And don't misunderstand me, honey: Caroline was nowhere near her first choice for me. She would have chosen somebody as white as the driven snow if she could have. But she couldn't. Because she only had two choices. She knew I've only wanted to marry two women in my entire life: you and Caroline. Those were her choices. You or Caroline. Caroline reentered the picture, so she cast her lot with Caro."

Gina shook her head. "What a narrow way to view human beings," she said. "And you really believe your own mother could be that hateful and cruel?"

"Yes," Dutch said. "She's that hateful and cruel. No doubt about it. I saw signs for years in the little comments she would make. But I just dismissed them. She was, at least I thought at that time, such a giving, caring woman. But when she met you, and I saw that hatred deep within her eyes, it couldn't be dismissed any longer. I knew on that day, when we left Nantucket, that she was my enemy. She was my mother, but she was my enemy. But even I never dreamed she'd take it to this level."

"She wants to destroy you now."

"She wants to destroy me. And probably you too," Dutch said, clutching his wife's hand tightly. "So brace yourself for more."

"I'm braced, don't worry," Gina said, and then she hesitated, wondered if now was the right time, decided that, *under the circumstances*, there would never be a right time. She exhaled. "The odd thing is," she said, "she had it all wrong."

Dutch looked at her. "My mother?"

"Yep. She wanted to break up our marriage so that I wouldn't conceive her grandchild," Gina said and looked at Dutch. "When I already have."

Dutch stared at his wife. Stared with a look of happiness, horror, joy and fear. "Are you saying that. . . that you're. . . that we're pregnant, Gina? Are you saying that we're pregnant?"

Gina nodded, tears coming to her eyes. "I found out the day of the State Dinner. I had planned to tell you later that night."

"How far along?"

"Five weeks."

Dutch stood up, Gina stood too, and they fell into each other's arms, with Dutch's eyes shut tight.

For the longest time they just stood there, oblivious to the world and the harshness that now surrounded them. It was, for both of them, the happiest news they could have ever received. And, *given the circumstances*, given their life in this fishbowl, the saddest.

Dutch pulled her back, his hands gripping her arms. "I'm so happy," he said with a smile. But he kept looking at her, and his look was more painful than joyous

"What is it?" Gina asked, already knowing the answer.

"We have nearly four years left in office," he said.

She nodded. "I know. I was taking birth control religiously when we first got married. Then so many things started happening all at once that I just stopped thinking about it. I'm so sorry, Dutch."

"And I'm so happy," Dutch said, managing to smile again despite his fears. "It's what I want so badly, Gina. A child. *Our* child. That will be the most beautiful thing, to have a child by the woman I love."

"But we'll have to raise our child in this place."

"Do we?" Dutch asked, his hands rubbing her arms, his stark green eyes flickering with so many possibilities that even he couldn't keep track.

Gina, however, couldn't even entertain the thought. "We can't quit, Dutch," she said.

A look so deflating came over Dutch that Gina wanted to cry. But then he nodded, because he knew she spoke the truth. "We will raise our child to be a wonderful citizen of the world," he said. "And we'll be wonderful parents." They both smiled. "But we'll do it our way. On our terms. No matter what."

Gina studied him. "Even if it means quitting?"

"Even if it means quitting. I have a responsibility to this country, and I have done and will continue to do all I can to fulfill that responsibility. But my first obligation is to you, and to our child."

Gina looked at him, and he looked at her, and both assumed what the other was thinking, but neither had the nerve to confirm it.

Because the world would take it the wrong way, and declare victory, and insist that they knew all along that a union like theirs could never take the heat. That a union like theirs would wither, would fall right off the vine, under the bright lens of scrutiny.

But the bright lens of Dutch's eyes saw it differently. Because this wasn't about the world. This wasn't about anybody scrutinizing anything about their relationship. This was about him and his wife. Their life. Their happiness. Their blessed child.

And in those matters of the heart the world and all its charges, countercharges, sex, lies, and videotape, didn't have a vote.

EIGHTEEN

The Washington press corps stood on the press pad on the southern end of the White House as the president and First Lady emerged from the portico. Looking comfortably attired in bright, casual clothing, the couple, hand in hand, made their way over to the pool of reporters anxiously waiting. The agreement was that one of them would ask all of the questions on behalf of the entire press pool, although they rarely kept to those agreements.

"Where are you going, Mr. President?" Andrew Singer, the designated reporter, asked.

"On vacation," Dutch answered.

"On vacation?" Singer asked as if he was stunned. "At a time like this?"

"Best time of the year to go."

"But, sir, you've been accused of sexually assaulting three women. Your own mother has come out in favor of the women and against you. There are criminal investigations underway. There's talk of Congress drafting articles of impeachment. And you're going on *vacation*?"

"Yes," Dutch said.

"But, sir, aren't you going to at least proclaim your innocence?"

"I'm innocent. There. I've proclaimed it."

"But that's not enough, sir," the reporter said.

Dutch and Gina laughed. "Why am I not surprised?" he asked.

"You two seem to be taking this very lightly, sir."

"Yes, we are. Aren't we?"

"But why?"

"Why not?"

The popular, but now frustrated reporter looked to his colleagues. Another reporter, Nora Tatem, took over.

"Why don't you proclaim your innocence, sir?" she said.

"Asked and answered," Dutch said.

"Is it because you're guilty?"

"Is that what it is, Nora? Gosh. Thank-you for pointing that out to me."

"That's what it appears to be."

"Appearances can be misleading."

"But why aren't you fighting back if you're so innocent?"

"I am."

"You're fighting back by going on vacation?"

"Precisely."

"But where are you going, sir?" she asked as if her colleague hadn't already asked it.

"On vacation," Dutch said again.

"But you can't just leave!"

Dutch looked at Gina, his face unable to stop grinning, although she could see the pain in his eyes. *The nerve of these people*, he wanted to say. "Watch me," he said instead, and he and his wife left the baffled press, walked up to the helipad, and boarded Marine One.

By the time the helicopter arrived at Andrews Air Force Base and they were boarding Air Force One, the cable news shows, as they predicted, were rerunning snippets of the interview and were livid with what their commentators viewed as the president's cavalier attitude.

First, there was the commentator on MSNBC, who couldn't get past the gaiety. "He should be pulling his hair out," the commentator insisted, "but he's laughing?"

Then the CNN commentator: "The evidence is too compelling. That videotape is too damning. You'd laugh too, if you had no defense."

Then FOX: "Dutch Harber is a disgrace to the office of the presidency and to the entire human race! He should do all of us a favor and resign right now rather than take this country through a protracted impeachment trial. Especially since we all already know he's guilty."

And the commentators on CNN and MSNBC agreed: the president is guilty as sin and should stop that grinning, and come out and confess.

By the time Air Force One had taxied the runway, ready to lift up and fly the friendly skies, the commentators had turned their aim away from Dutch, and were now pointing it squarely at Gina.

"She'll leave him for certain now," a tall, thin woman on MSNBC predicted. "Black women don't put up with that mess."

"Oh, she'll leave," said an anchor on FOX. "No doubt about that. Her feminist bona fides won't allow her to stay. Her independent, *I am woman,* superficial pride wouldn't bear for her to be viewed as some stand by her man lovesick female."

And a talking head on CNN summed it up this way: "With that videotape, with that level of evidence, she's definitely leaving," he assured the public. "That marriage is over!"

And Dutch and Gina sat back on Air Force One, still holding hands, still staring at that CNN commentator, a man they didn't know and had never even met, confidently inform the American people of the demise of their marriage. And if it wasn't so sad, they'd be rolling in the aisles with laughter.

But it was sad. And therefore they just sat.

Nathan Riles escorted Roman Wilkes into the morning room where Victoria Harber was waiting. As soon as she saw him, she smiled.

"Hello there," Victoria said.

"Hello," Roman said. She was wearing, he noticed, a very revealing peignoir, which looked ridiculous on her. But she was on top of the world right now. Was the woman who had brought a president to his knees. The fact that the president in question also happened to be her son seemed beside the point to her. She was flying high. She undoubtedly figured she could wear, and could have,

Roman thought as he sat down beside her, anything and anyone she wanted.

"I hear you've been a busy man."

"How so?"

"I understand you're all in, that you've informed your girlfriend that you will definitely defend her brother the murderer."

"Ex-girlfriend, and that's right. I am officially defending Marcus Rance. Why, you want to contribute to his legal defense?"

"Don't be absurd! I have an image to uphold! You may not take yours seriously, but my image is above reproach." Then she looked at him. "Do you have them?" she asked him.

He reached into his suit coat pocket and pulled out an envelope. Gave it to her.

"Why are you giving them to me? Why haven't I seen them on the news yet? The timing would be impeccable."

"Kick'em while they're down, something like that?" Roman asked.

"Exactly like that," Victoria said. "And I'm enjoying every minute of it. You can always count on the press to take whatever red meat you throw their way and chew it up until it's only worth spitting out."

"I thought you'd like to see the goods first," Roman said. "To make sure they live up to your standards so there'll be no issues with me getting the second half of my pay."

"Are they suggestive?" Victoria asked as she began to peel open the envelope. "Do they show you and that Regina woman hugging and kissing as if she's turned the nation's White House into her own crack house for sexual deviants?"

"Hugging and kissing my ass," Roman said. "The brother is making love in those photographs." Roman said this as Victoria, now excited, pulled out the photographs. "And he's making love to you," he then added.

Victoria rose from her seat with the agility of a woman half her age as soon as she saw, not a photo of a naked Roman Wilkes making love to a naked Regina Lansing, but a naked Nathan Riles making love to his long-time employer, and lover, Victoria Harber.

"Yeah," Roman said with laughter. "I thought that would get a rise out of you."

Victoria's mouth flew open as she flipped through photograph after photograph, sexual encounter after sexual encounter. She looked up at Roman, stupefied, and then back at the photos, as if she had been mistaken, as if she couldn't possibly be seeing what she was seeing.

"But how could you know," she started. She and Nathan never shared their relationship with anyone, not ever! It was forbidden for him to so much as mention her name out of the context of his job!

She looked at Roman again. "Where did you get these?" she demanded to know.

"That's my business. But this is what's going to happen," Roman said, his face now serious, unrepentant. "You and your three musketeers will go back on television, admit that all y'all lied through y'all teeth, and beg the president's forgiveness. Period. If that doesn't happen, if you can't get those ladies to recant, I will whip out the photographs and show for all the world to see you, Victoria Harber, that great bastion of rich, white propriety, fucking the help."

Victoria stumbled back, and then sat down.

Roman stared at her. "How's that for upholding that above reproach image of yours?" he asked.

She was still too stunned to speak.

"I mean, who knows?" he went on. "Those old racist biddies that you run with might understand. They might, in fact, be doing the same thing themselves. But then again, hypocrisy is a bitch, isn't it? It never wants to admit its own failings. Nope, with this kind of proof you'll be castigated, lady. Ostracized. Eliminated from every sewing circle, every country club you're a member of. You'll be all on your own."

Victoria was speechless. For the first time in her life she was speechless.

"Those photos will always be my trump card," Roman continued. "And if anything happens to me, and it's some funny-bunny stuff going on with the way I kick the bucket, they will become public. So you see, Mrs. Harber, you're screwed no matter who you fuck."

Victoria closed her eyes, disgusted by his terminology.

Roman, however, couldn't care less about her disgust. He kept pounding. "But if you don't want to spend the rest of your days alone, isolated and ostracized, not to mention laughed at for the sheer magnitude of your hypocrisy, then you had better get those recantations. Because unlike you and that little three-ring circus you displayed, I know how to put on a show. And it'll be compared to the greatest show on earth when I leave that stage." Then Roman smiled. "We understand each other. Don't we?"

But she didn't. She just couldn't understand any of it. "But I paid you to get with Regina," she said. "I promised you another half million dollars if you delivered took photographs of you and her. But instead you seek to embarrass *me*?"

"Exactly."

"But *why*?" Victoria asked, confused to a point that bordered on panic.

"For one thing," Roman said, "I have a conscience. Unlike you, Mrs. Harber, I care which end of that horizontal line I spend eternity. And for another thing, I happen to be eternally fond of the very woman you hate. Because I love Regina Lansing. She's my girl and always will be. And I get really annoyed when somebody tries to hurt her. I get super annoyed by that. And because Dutch Harber is her man now, and she obviously loves the man, I get equally perturbed when people try to run him down too. Because that was what you tried to do with your own son, Mrs. Harber. You tried to knock him

242

down. A hit and run if ever there was a hit and run! But you didn't see my black ass coming. Did you?" Roman said this with a grin. "But I'll bet you see me now."

He grabbed his briefcase. "I'll keep that five-hundred grand," he said, "for my expenses. But the second part of my *payment*?" He grinned. "I think you ought to hold on to that. Don't want to be considered a greedy man."

He left the room, although Victoria, still reeling, didn't even know he had gone.

He was, in fact, just about to let himself out of the mansion's front door when Nathan Riles, Victoria's trusted manservant for over forty years, in additional to his *other* duties, met him at the exit. And handed him a DVD.

"Give it to the press," Nathan said.

"What is it that I'm giving to the press?" Roman wanted to know.

"The tape of that night in the White House. The one with the president and Caroline Parker. Not the doctored one, not the one with the missing scenes. This is the original."

Roman stared at Nathan, at this black man nearly thirty years his senior. "I just laid those photos on her, man," he said. "She will most likely fire you when she discovers that you were the one who gave them to me. Not to mention when she discovers you gave me this tape."

"She won't fire me," Nathan said confidently. "She won't even suspect me. She'll believe somebody broke into this Fort Knox fortified mansion and snapped those photos, and then broke back out, before she suspects me. I'm an old black dumbass far as she's concerned. Good for a little sex and a little cleaning, nothing else. What harm could little ol' stupid me possibly do?"

Roman stared at him. "Why do you put up with it, man?"

Nathan hesitated, exhaled, and then looked away. "It's complicated," he said.

And Roman knew that it was. This man, this servant, truly loved that hateful woman. And whenever her hate strayed too far from home and sought to destroy others, he would undoubtedly step in, behind her back, and right the ship again.

That was why Roman never fell in love with any woman beyond Regina. You had to pretend that you were damn near blind to overlook all of their glaring faults.

And Roman was too visual to ever do that.

He shook Nathan's hand, pocketed the tape, and left.

When the story broke it broke big, becoming as sensational a worldwide media event as the original accusations. Allison, LaLa, and Christian, along with a slew of other staff and cabinet officials, jammed into the Roosevelt Room to watch the rapidly unfolding story.

First there was the president's mother. She didn't stand behind any podium this time, didn't have any standing room only crowd around her. She, instead, stood in the library of her home, a solitary figure, reading from a shaking piece of paper:

"It is with a profound sense of conviction that I must come forward and tell the truth. No-one is coercing me to come forward; no-one is threatening me in any way. I come forward because I can no longer live with what I've uncovered. To my horror, I've discovered that I was used to get to my son. I've discovered that the accusations made by Caroline Parker, Jennifer Caswell, and Katherine Marris against my son, the president, are totally false."

She looked up from the paper when she said this. Then she looked back down. "They all made up these stories of rape to bring the president down. None of these stories are true in the least. None of them. They made them up because they wanted to destroy my son, and they came to me because they knew I did not approve of my son's marriage to Regina Lansing. A marriage of which I still do not approve."

She looked up again, as if to add emphasis to her point. "I would hope, in time, that my son will be able to forgive me for believing these women. Right now, I just want to be left alone, to live my remaining years in peace and tranquility. That's why I came forward. To clear the slate. To make it clear that what they did was horrible, and because I believed them, I deserve the estrangement from my son my actions have caused."

Then she folded up her little paper, continued to stare at the camera, and then the screen faded to black.

"Oh, so she's the innocent victim now?" LaLa said.

"Who cares," Allison said, grinning. "She came clean. And you know the media is going to play it up big."

"They'd better," LaLa said, standing up. "Or I'll be out there playing it up. Those women lied, that's all they need to say."

And just like that the headlines shifted from the president's certain guilt, to the certain guilt of the three women, known now as the Harber Three.

First, Jennifer Caswell went before the cameras, insisting that everything Victoria Harber said was pure fabrication and her story, including her original cry of rape, was the honest truth. The president's henchmen, she said, had gotten to his mother, had, in her words, "scared that poor old lady," and that was why she recanted.

Next hour came Kate Marris, as she went before the cameras to disassociate herself from Victoria's remarks also. She never lies, she told the eager press, and this time was no exception. Dutch Harber had raped her, and she was sticking by her story.

Then it was Caroline Parker's time. She had no idea why Victoria Harber would have recanted the truth, but that tape didn't lie.

As she was speaking on CNN and FOX, however, MSNBC was playing the original tape, the one that showed Dutch Harber, not raping Caroline Parker, but waking up horrified that she was in his bed, and tossing her out of it.

And that was when the coverage took yet another dramatic turn. As the days proceeded, the story became all about the women, their backgrounds, their lies. And then the authorities got involved as one by one they were led away in handcuffs, for lying to federal agents, for other high crimes and misdemeanors.

Even the president's mother, who many talking heads on the cable news channels had assumed would be given a pass, wasn't given anything, and was also forced to do the perp walk to the jail house for all the world to see. She, too, had lied to federal agents, none of whom were buying her *I was duped* defense. Especially after that tape surfaced. She would be released on her own recognizance a mere few hours later, but it still made for must-see TV.

The hours and days that followed had Kate Marris blaming the president's mother, accusing her of taking advantage of her love for Dutch and paying her to lie.

Caroline Parker complained that she was promised a million dollars by Victoria Harber also, but hadn't seen a dime of that money. She, to the amazement of the press, was considering a lawsuit.

Jennifer Caswell, who told one talk show that Victoria had promised her money too, although she insisted, on a different show, that she never said that, sold her story to the tabloids. *Longer, Thicker, and Juicier Than Any I've Ever Had*, was the headline, and it was such an incredible way to describe the President of the United States, that it made even the Financial Times of London.

Then the story took yet another turn and the recantations turned into recriminations by the same commentators who had earlier judged the president guilty.

"The Speaker of the House owes the president an apology," one bellowed.

"The Speaker should resign," bellowed another one.

Then the commentaries became all about how supportive of the president they were all along, with the truth of the matter buried by the weight of their own contorted realities:

"I said from day one that we shouldn't rush to judgment our great president."

"I knew that tape was doctored!"

"What impeachment? Who said anything about impeachment?"

And the CNN commentator who had declared the Harbers' marriage over, said this: "That marriage is strong. I knew all along it could withstand any controversy." And the same man added: "Why is the president still on vacation? Why isn't he addressing the American people and thanking them for standing by him?"

Far away from the maddening crowd, they lay in the hotel bed, with Dutch on his back and Gina on top of him, his penis thrusting into her in long slides along her saturated walls. Gina sat upright, her hands behind her on his knees, her breast flapping against her chest as she began to ride him hard. Dutch grabbed her breasts and squeezed them, rubbed her bulbs and squeezed them, as his penis moved in deeper and deeper with her every gallop. Although the television was still on, and they could hear all of the chatter of the ever-breaking, ever-changing, shameless press accounts, they kept fucking; they kept moaning and groaning and enjoying each other, as if all of that hoopla had nothing to do with them.

They were in Miami Beach, in the very hotel where they had first met eleven long years ago, in the very room where he first made love to her. Now she was making love to him, and he was so grateful to her for sticking by him, even before the release of that non-doctored tape, even before his mother's recantation and even Jennifer's first rape allegation to begin this madness, that he reached up, pulled her down on top of him, and wrapped her tightly in his arms. And his slow motion thrusts got fast.

He thrust into her and thrust into her, his penis penetrating so deeply that was able to take swipe after swipe of the back of her vagina, causing her to nearly scream just from the intense feeling of it.

For the longest time he held her, and fucked her, his penis so lubricated with her juices that he couldn't help but hit her in just the right spot every time he moved in any direction.

And then, just as Dutch had released and they were both in the throes of an electrifying orgasm; just as he had stopped thrusting to hold her tightly to his body; just as they both squeezed out the last of that incredible feeling of ecstasy, of romance, of love, and they collapsed onto the bed still in each other's arms; just then, it came. The big news that stopped all of the other big news in its tracks:

"Socialite and philanthropist Victoria Harber, the mother of the President of the United States, died this morning of a massive heart attack. She died alone in her mansion. She was sixty-four years old."

For a moment, Dutch and Gina stopped too. And then Dutch sat up, with Gina still on his lap, and turned the television set up louder.

The newscast spoke of her years as the daughter of a millionaire, the heiress to a fortune in her own right, and then her marriage to the president's father. They spoke of all of her charitable work on behalf of the poor, especially the poor in Africa. They showed her feeding the little black babies, fanning flies from the faces of pot-bellied children, standing in a hot warehouse giving Christmas gifts to America's poor.

And they showed various photographs of Victoria Harber throughout her life, from her youth onward, all pictures of a very beautiful woman whose once smiling eyes seemed to turn harder and colder with each passing winter. By the time of her death, the last picture they showed, she looked like nothing but a shell of the girl she used to be: hard, cold, and aloof.

And then they showed her mug shot.

Gina watched Dutch as he watched those photographs, as he saw the highlights of his mother's life in sixty seconds. And he should have felt sad. He should have felt pain. He should have felt an emptiness inside of him that no-one in this world could fill. But all he could feel was remorse. Not for anything he did to her, he could honestly say that he never did anything that he shouldn't have done to his mother. But his remorse was for what she, with her bitterness, with her hatred, had done to herself.

"It's as if she was already dead," he said. "I think she died to me when I took you meet her and she showed me her true self for the first time. She showed me, not just her bad side, but all of the ugly layers of that bad side. And she froze in my mind. She ceased to be my mother at that moment in time."

"But at least she seemed to be trying to make amends," Gina said. "She did confess that those women lied."

"After claiming she was duped, yeah, if you want to call it a confession."

"Maybe she was trying to gain a conscience."

But Dutch shook his head. "Nope, I don't believe that."

"You don't believe it?"

"Not for a second. Not that woman. Somebody got to her. And from what I could find out, which wasn't a whole lot, that somebody just may have been your friend."

"*My* friend?" Gina asked, puzzled. "LaLa?"

"Roman Wilkes," Dutch said and then looked at Gina, to see her reaction. Roman Wilkes was a very attractive man who was still, Dutch believed, very much attracted to his wife.

"Wilkie?" Gina said in disbelief. "You think Wilkie got your mother to recant? But why? How?"

"I haven't worked out the how. But Nathan Riles tells me that he did indeed meet with my mother, and that, although he doesn't know himself just what the Intel was, it was powerful enough that when Wilkes left, mother was quite shaken."

"Nathan Riles?" Gina asked with a frown. "Who's Nathan Riles?"

"He works for my mother. He's been with our family for most of my life."

"And he saw Wilkie visit her?"

"Yes. He saw all of them visit. Roman Wilkes, Max, all of the women too."

Again, Gina was puzzled. "Why would Max be visiting her? You told him to?"

"He was scheming with her, no doubt. He has an ambition to run for some political office and mother probably intended to provide financial backing. Provided, of course, he did her bidding."

"But what could he do to help her?"

"Provide the camera that filmed my encounter with Caroline, for one thing."

Gina looked at him. "Are you serious?"

"I can't prove it, but I certainly believe it."

"Then why haven't you fired his ass?"

"Because I can't prove it yet. But when I do, I'll take care of Max. But Nathan tends to keep me posted with the goings on around mother's estate." Then he exhaled. "It's his now."

"The house in Nantucket?"

"Yes. He had to deal with my mother for forty-some-odd years. He deserves it."

"Amen," Gina said, unable to imagine anybody putting up with that woman that long.

"And now she's gone," Dutch said, exhaling.

Gina studied him. "It doesn't hurt you on any level?"

"It hurts. I did love her. Even respected and admired her once upon a time. But it just doesn't sting the way it should. She's gone. May God have mercy on her soul. But I don't know what else I can say."

"You'll need to get to Nantucket and make the arrangements."

"Or let Nathan do it."

"But you can't ask him to arrange your mother's funeral," Gina said. "I think giving him that estate, and I would hope the finances to help him run it, is a great thing. But she was your mother, Dutch. You're her only child. You have to do it. It's only right."

Dutch smiled, pulled Gina into his arms. "And you're right of course. Yes, I'll take care of the arrangements. But I'm glad the truth came out before she died. And I'm also grateful to your friend. He may have saved my bacon."

"Isn't that something? Way to go, Wilkie. He always was an oddball. But why would he do it?"

"I can only guess," Dutch said. "He didn't tell me a thing. Nathan had to give me the heads up."

"So why do you think he did it?"

"Because of you. Because that man is still in love with you."

"Oh, Dutch," Gina said dismissively, "I'm sure that's not it."

"Don't you *oh, Dutch* me! I'll bet that is it. But he can forget that. You are so off market, lady, that there's no longer any market to be off of!"

"What?" Gina asked with a grin. "Even you don't know what that means."

"It means," Dutch said, serious now, "that I love you and I'll not stand idly by for any man to so much as think about getting a piece of you. They can't have even a taste. Not even Roman Wilkes. Although I did phone and tell him how grateful I am for all of his assistance."

Gina looked at him. "You spoke to him?"

Dutch nodded. "We spoke."

"And he admitted being the person who encouraged your mother to change her story?"

"He didn't admit it. But he didn't deny it, either. He just told me to tell you to keep your chin up, that it'll get better before it gets worse, and that he's still working his butt off on behalf of Marcus Rance."

"Which will only mean more headaches for you, especially when the press gets wind of the fact that you're bankrolling his defense and that my ex-lover is his attorney. They are going to have a field day with that one."

Dutch snorted. "I kind of think I'm used to it by now." Gina smiled. "Besides, what do they want from us? Do they want us to sit by and let an innocent man rot in prison until I'm out of office, or do the right thing despite how it polls?"

"Let him rot, of course," Gina said and Dutch smiled. Then he moved her back on top of him. "And now," he said, "it's about time you show me if you've learned anything at all in the eleven years since I first blew your mind in this very room."

"But Dutch," Gina said, amazed at his stamina, "I just showed you."

"Show me again," he said, looking at her lips and then kissing them. "And again," he said, still kissing her. "And again."

"Don't you think, given the news of your mother's passing, we should, you know?"

"What?" Dutch asked, puzzled. "We should what?"

"Ease up, Dutch. Out of respect."

"Respect for her? But we didn't respect her."

Gina smiled. "You know what I mean!"

Dutch nodded. He knew. He wrapped her in his arms.

Then he looked at her. "Ready to go back?"

"Back to the pettiness and the hypocrisies and the complaints about my clothes and my hair and my speech and why I'm so focused on the poor and not on the middle class? Go back there? Ah, let me see: No."

"Then you know what that means?"

"What?"

"More of this," he said, rolled her over onto her back, and began kissing her.

As he moved on top of her, however, he reached over to the nightstand, grabbed the TV's remote, and with all of that Washington chatter still ringing in his ears, shut the whole thing off.

EPILOGUE

Seven Months Later

The crowds were in the thousands by the time the Harbers prepared to leave the hospital. The city of Newark was still amazed that the First Lady of the United States would choose their still-struggling but beloved city, and her hometown, as the place for her baby to come into this world. Although neither she nor the president would admit it publicly, everybody who had an opinion believed that they did not want their child to ever have to say that he was born in the Beltway.

Dutch sat in the corner of the hospital room holding his son with the nervousness of a brand new dad, and with the assuredness of a determined father. Every time he looked down at his tiny seven pound frame; at his big hazel eyes and little button nose; at his mother's ears and forehead and his lips; and every time he smelled his wonderful baby smell, he wanted to cry.

He had a son? Really? This was *his* boy? It still seemed surreal.

And that was why he couldn't stop praying. That was why he couldn't stop thinking about the awesome responsibility he now had for this tiny little baby.

Walter Robert Harber, Jr. Robert they would call him. Or Bobby, Gina had said.

And Dutch looked back down at the baby. And prayer some more. He prayed that he would get this right. He prayed that he wouldn't be too tough on the boy, that Gina wouldn't baby him, that they would somehow manage, even their clumsiness, to get it just right. He looked at Gina, who was standing on the side of the bed, her baby bags all packed and ready to go. Looking like a kid herself. And Dutch smiled. Because he knew now, not the night he became President of the United States, not the night he won reelection, but even when he married Gina. But he knew now, at this very moment, in this hospital in this struggling, wonderful city, that he was above all men the most richly blessed.

After Gina complained no end about their requirement that she ride a wheelchair downstairs, despite LaLa and Christian's pleads, she ultimately agreed to ride down on the elevator and then get out and walk.

"Thank-you," LaLa said, moving over to Dutch and looking at the beautiful baby that would become her godchild. Christian looked too, and although he was slated to be the godfather, he felt more like the big brother than anything paternal. But he smiled, said his goo-goo-ga-ga's and stood beside Dutch.

And then all of them, Dutch, Gina, Robert, LaLa and Christian, and the contingent of agents, made their way onto the elevator and after Gina got out of the wheelchair, out of the hospital. The Secret

Service had wanted them to go out a back way, away from the crowd that kept on swelling. But Dutch had said no.

These people, mostly poor, mostly happy black faces, were the people he represented. The real America, not that plastic society they had to deal with.

And he wasn't running away from them.

The festive crowd went wild as soon as the happy couple appeared. And as soon as they realized the president was carrying the baby, they became nearly hysterical. Hundreds of cameras flashed as they all tried to take pictures of the newborn even though the perimeter the Secret Service had set up was too far away, and the president had the baby too snuggled, for them to be successful. But they tried anyway.

Dutch grinned and Gina waved as they moved slowly toward the limo, the baby beginning to cry at the terrible sounds of the new, ear shattering cheers. And Dutch wanted to tell him to get used to it. But he only looked down at him and smiled. Don't worry, he wanted to say. These are the good guys.

LaLa offered to take the baby with her in the car that she, Christian and other staff were riding in, but Dutch refused the offer. This baby, his eyes made clear, would be raised by him and Gina, not by aides, nannies, or other assorted people. LaLa smiled, because she knew exactly what he meant, and headed for her awaiting limo.

And when Dutch, Gina, and Robert got into their limo, and Robert took his tiny fingers and wrapped them around his father's big finger, seemingly holding on for dear life, Dutch did cry. He let the tears roll. Gina looked at him, looked at the death grip the baby had on Dutch's finger, and wanted to cry too.

Because nothing was more beautiful to a couple that was supposedly always surrounded by it, than a gesture that was so common, so expected and predictable, until it was, because of its simplicity, the most beautiful of all.

Dutch looked out at the glowing crowd, a crowd that seemed to love them. And he loved them back, if only for that moment, because they were the everyday people, the heart and soul of America. And even when he saw a smattering of distractors, with signs that read, *Those Women Told the Truth*, or compared the president to Hitler, he still was the happiest man alive.

Before the limo doors were closed, a reporter in the front of the rope line was able to shout out if the president was sorry that his mother didn't live to see her only grandchild. And Dutch, without hesitation, yelled out, "no," unsure if the reporter heard him or not.

Gina looked at him. "That was so not politically correct," she said as the baby grabbed her finger too.

"I know," Dutch said, looking up at Gina's radiant face, and then down at the baby, a baby who already had them wrapped around his fingers. And Dutch couldn't stop grinning. "Isn't it great?" he asked.

And Gina grinned too, because it really was great. Because they had decided, for the sake of the child, for the sake of the office Dutch had sworn to uphold, that they would not quit. But they also decided that they would live on their own terms. On this they stood firm. And if Washington didn't like it, if the American public didn't like it, if Congress had problems with it, then they could always force them out.

But in the meantime they would move along at their own pace, as a threesome now, accustomed to the cheers and jeers of the crowd, the ups and downs of the polls, the shouts and yells of reporters, as the doors of the limousine shut out the noise, and they were ushered, kicking and screaming and laughing from ear to ear, back into the fishbowl.

ABOUT THE AUTHOR

Mallory Monroe is the bestselling author of numerous novels, including The President's Girlfriend, Romancing the Mob Boss, Mob Boss 2: The Heart of the Matter, Romancing Her Protector, Romancing the Bulldog, and If You Wanted the Moon.

Visit

www.austinbrookpublishing.com

for more information on all of her titles

Made in the USA
Lexington, KY
14 March 2013